I'M AFLOAT, I'M AFLOAT:

OR,

RODERICK THE ROVER.

A ROMANCE.

LONDON:

PUBLISHED BY G. PURKESS, COMPTON STREET, SOHO.

PREFACE.

THE place and the period selected for illustration throughout a great portion of the following pages are sufficiently distinguished in authentic history to claim the reader's earnest attention. The creeks and harbours of the West India Islands have in former days been the scene of so many wonderful incidents in the lives of those adventurous and daring spirits, the buccaneers, that the writer who is conversant with existing records, has little occasion to draw upon his imagination for pictures of the wild and the romantic. The reader must not, therefore, reject as unworthy of belief the most striking features of the following tale, merely because the even tenor of modern life is but seldom chequered by similarly exciting adventures.

Neither are the circumstances under which Lord Withingham abandoned the paternal halls, and became a rover of the sea, so unparalleled by more recent instances as to exceed the bounds of credibility. The annals of more than one noble English house, if truly read, would afford events as strange and startling, but which the prudence or family pride of the illustrious adventurers have kept profoundly secret hitherto from public ken.

The genius of Byron was required to throw a charm around the character of the Greek pirate, Conrad,—

" Linked with one virtue and a thousand crimes."

But the hero of our tale is no such atrocious personage. The buccaneer of that period must not be confounded with the blood-thirsty, cruel and rapacious pirate. The one devoted his arms to a contest with the vessels of one hated power only, while the black flag directed its agressions against the peaceful merchants of the world at large. Though our Roderick was dauntless in the fight, he was ever ready to stay the effusion of blood, and put a stop to unnecessary violence ; and when circumstances allowed him once more to tread his native shores, we find him gladly abandoning scenes where little more than infamy was to be gained, to pass the remainder of his days in the domestic and social duties dear to the patriot's heart.

The love of Lord William for the " high-born Spanish ladye " is an interesting episode. We must not judge the warm-hearted daughter of the sunny south by the same starched rules that envelope society in our colder latitudes ; but admit at once that " love at first sight " never had a fairer justification than in the personal graces of our hero and the Lady Ida.

We need not dilate upon the lesser characters in the story, but leave it trustingly to the ordeal of that public criticism to which all must bow ; hoping to secure the approbation which is the author's most highly esteemed reward.

London, December, 1847.

I'M AFLOAT, I'M AFLOAT:

OR,

CHAPTER I.

FREEBOOTERS' RETREAT.—MODE OF FIGHT.—DESCRIPTION OF RODERICK.

BETWEEN the harbour of Matanzas and that of Havana, on the northern shores of the island of Cuba, there is a deep, still, narrow river, that indents the coast for a distance of some two miles, watering a most beautiful valley in its course, locked in by gentle eminences, scarcely meriting the name of mountains, there is such a lack of abruptness, such a gradual and almost imperceptible rise in the elevations. At the mouth of the river, where it empties into the Gulf of Mexico, there is now located a strong and well-constructed fort, garrisoned by the Spanish troops, which the policy of the home government supplies in liberal numbers. At the date of our story no fort was there, but the river and the fertile valley that it watered were the stronghold of a daring rover. The ruins of his stone battery are still visible, and are pointed out to the curious just at the head of the navigable part of the river, and the Spanish and creole planters, who now improve the rich soil in the neighbourhood, relate to the stranger thrilling stories, illustrative of the daring character of this rover of the gulf. They will point out to you spots from whence rich treasures have been recovered in modern times, being the secreted booty, or portions of it, belonging to the early occupants of the valley. The leader of the freebooters is called by them Roderick the Rover, in the wild and romantic stories they relate of him; and the character he possessed, as evinced by these tales, was that of a singularly brave and chivalrous disposition, so mingled with a desire for plunder or revenge upon the Spaniards, that, in place of becoming a hero, as the champion of some nation, by fighting for her interest under a recognised flag, he preferred to own the name of pirate—be his own master—and set the world at defiance. For years, he was the terror of all Spaniards who navigated these seas. He disclaimed all connection with the buccaniers and freebooters, whose principal haunts were on the Tortugas, nor would he ever join in their combined operations, wherein they won such surprising victories, and gained such enormous wealth. In vain was he solicited to join with them in their attacks upon various settlements, such as Maracaibo, St. Augustine, City of San Pedro, Porto Bello, and, in short, the sacking of all the rich possessions of the Spaniards, whether among the isles of the West Indies, or on the main land. He turned from all these seductive invitations, and pursued his profession of a rover singly and alone in his favourite craft.

It was his strict rule never to commit violence on any save the Spaniards, unless he was first opposed by them—and then his resentment was fearful. He declared open war against the commerce of Spain, and against her alone.

His crew of desperadoes loved while they feared him, for to them, though he was stern in the maintenance of the most unyielding discipline, yet he was rigidly just and honest as to the sharing of booty; and still further to gain him the right of command, a regular monthly stipend was agreed upon and paid by their commander to every man.

To be sure, these men were chosen from the fearful and daring spirits of the times, and the sixteenth and seventeenth centuries teemed with such, but they were chosen ones, nevertheless; for Roderick must know a man before he would enlist him, and so high was his service held among the freebooters of isles, that he was never at a loss for a full complement of men, and, indeed, he was not unfrequently obliged to refuse admittance to tried and approved ones. The main reason of this was the chivalrous character of his warfare; for while the buccaniers generally had grown so lawless as to take prizes from all nations, Roderick strictly adhered to his original design of preying upon the Spanish only, and for this purpose had even taken out letters of marque.

So notorious had Roderick become, that several vessels had been fitted out in Spain, and sent to take him at all hazards, but they never returned! and the government, at last, resorted to the singular expedient of promulgating among the pirates who infested the island, that any one who should betray Roderick, the Rover should receive full pardon from the crown for all past offences, however heinous, with full absolution from the pope, and a regal fortune for life.

This was a rich offer, indeed, but the government knew full well that it must be a tempting bait that could allure men who already revelled in wealth; but, after all, they did not know the men they had to deal with, for, though following a trade of the most reckless and unlawful character, yet they seemed to be endowed with the most intuitive horror of treachery, or betrayal of each other's interests; and so well was this trait in their character tested and known, that it was not an unfrequent simile of the seventeenth century, in Europe, to say, "as faithful as a buccanier."

And thus, in spite of the most cunning devices and stratagems, and all the open force that was sent to combat him, Roderick managed for years to keep the sea in the most thorough-found and effective condition, and might honestly be said to have been master of the gulf.

Even his lawless neighbours, the freebooters, bore a degree of respect and fear for him, inasmuch as he had more than once forced them to own his superior power by positive trial; but they left him alone to pursue his own plans unmolested, and without the fear of successful opposition.

We have preferred thus to open directly and at once upon the theme of our tale, believing the reader would be sooner interested, than through the means of a long and glowing introduction, relating to climate and scenery, as is the usual mode; and following up this purpose, we shall trim our sails for a working passage.

One fair afternoon in May, there might be seen lying just off the mouth of the river we have described, a low, dark, rakish-looking craft, with roguery written in every line; and it needed no prophetic eye to tell the beholder that she was a vessel of a most suspicious character. She had three masts, and was rigged like a topsail schooner of the present day, save that she carried an extra jib, and a short mast stepped just on the quarter-deck, near the taffrail, on which might be spread a spencer and gaff-topsail, calculated to drive the hull with more speed through the water, and also to make her more weatherly, by crowding her bows close on the wind.

The craft, as she lay there upon the quiet waters of the Mexican gulf, seemed to be sleeping, so close did she appear to lie to the element that was her home. She was painted black fore and aft, larboard and starboard, masts, spars, everything was as black as night. She was long and sharp at the bows like a wedge, with high bulwarks, and a look altogether as though she had a contract with the elements that would enable her to make just such speed through the water as she might happen to desire.

As she lay there close off to the shore, her sails were all neatly brailed; but an experienced eye would have detected the fact that this had been so arranged, that a prompt effort would cover her with canvass as speedily as a sea-bird could spread his wing and lift himself for flight.

The extraordinary symmetry of her build, the faultless arrangement of the smallest rope, the knowing way that she rode by a single anchor, her peculiar hue of darkness, all combined to mark the beautiful tri-masted schooner as a pirate! Suddenly, as if by a charm, the topsails fell together, the fore and main-sails dropped from their brails, the jibs were hoisted, the spencer and gaff-topsail expanded at once, and the black craft bent gracefully under the pressure of this broad spread of canvass, while her bow were turned seaward, towards a dark speck upon the distant waters. Each moment added to her motion, until she seemed rather to skim over the ripling waves, than to cut her way through them, though a mound of foam lay constantly under her fore foot.

Her decks, before so still and quiet, were now peopled by scores of sturdy forms engaged in various duties about the vessel's gear; every sail was trimmed to a nicety, every rope was made fast where it should be, and the craft was a perfect picture of nautical beauty.

Before the vessel that had thus spread her broad wings, and flown quietly away, had reached a great distance from the land, the steady military roll of the drum that beats a crew to quarters came ominously across the sea, and those who remained upon the shore knew that the rover had called his people to their arms. In the meantime, that which appeared to be a mere speck in the horizon had now grown in form, and as it apparently rose out of the sea, it was easy to discover that it was a ponderous Spanish galleon of the largest class, with some of those prominent signs about her that bespoke a mingling of the man-of-war and merchant ship together.

She wore the blazoned flag of Spain at her gaff, and came on fearlessly, confident in her own strength, either to repel or conquer the piratical craft that they now discovered to be making for them, with the speed of the wind. The Spaniard did not vary his course a single point, but held it bravely, while the rover bore steadily and swiftly down upon the galleon.

There is something very fine in watching two vessels approach each other at sea under ordinary circumstances, but when with hostile intentions, it is peculiarly exciting.

The busy stir upon the Spaniard's deck showed that he was preparing for a warm contest, and with a determination of purpose, too, that bespoke cool and daring courage. Still they neared each other without any other visible tokens of hostility; and the rover seemed about to pass the galleon unharmed, when suddenly the helm was put up, and she shot athwart the Spaniard's stern so close that a biscuit might have been tossed from one to the other.

"What do you want, there, on my quarter?" hailed the Spanish captain.

"Haul down your flag!" was the prompt reply from the rover.

"Never! Keep off, or I will sink you to the bottom of the gulf."

"Starboard a little—so—steady," said Roderick the Rover, as his beautiful craft shot along side by side with the unwilling Spaniard; "heave the grapnels—make fast there, forward—lively—with a will, men!"

Already had the Spanish commander commenced a fierce and destructive fire upon his enemy's deck, but not a shot was returned, to the no small wonder of their enemies.

The rover issued his orders with the same calmness, as though he had been on a mere pleasure excursion—his men were formed in their divisions, and the captain of the galleon saw that the favourite mode of warfare among the rovers was about to be adopted, which was to carry their enemy by boarding, and a hand-to-hand contest, wherein their headlong and reckless bravery was sure to carry the day. It was too late for them to prevent this now, but preparations were instantly made to give them a warm reception.

Practised in this mode of warfare, the crew of the schooner clambered up the sides and rigging of the galleon, like so many monkeys, or leaped on to the deck from their own spars, until there were fifty men at the back of Roderick, armed to the teeth, following their leader, who cut his way through the Spanish crew to the quarter deck.

No power on earth could withstand the rovers after they had once gained footing on an enemy's deck in numbers—their headlong and impetuous courage knew no check. They paused for nothing—knew nothing, save success; and having been drilled to and experienced in this mode of warfare, they soon caused the haughty Spaniards to haul down their flag, and beg for quarter.

No sooner was the ensign of his enemy lowered, than Roderick sprang upon the quarter deck of the galleon, and, in a voice that reached the ears of all, he said,—

"The man who strikes another blow makes an enemy of me!"

These words acted like magic upon the fierce buccaniers that he had led to victory. The uplifted sword was stayed, the dagger fell harmless, the fierce grasp was relinquished, and for a moment the stillness of death reigned in place of the fierce din of the battle—even the wounded and dying seemed to pause in their groans to learn the purpose of the rover captain.

He was a noble figure, light and graceful in every limb, yet powerful in physical strength; his face was classically beautiful, and the dark raven hair that hung in richness about his neck, agreed with the piercing black of his handsome eye; over his lip curled a thin, silky moustache, the dark black of its hue contrasting richly with the pure olive of his complexion. His costume was of green velvet, trimmed with gold lace, the upper portion being a short spencer or jacket, elaborately wrought with gold cord and ornamented with golden buttons. His shirt was open at the throat, narrowed, and lay gracefully on the edge of his jacket collar. On his head he wore a richly ornamented boarding-cap, with a hanging tassel of gold cord. A narrow belt, clasped by a buckle of pure metal, supported the scabbard of his sword, and a brace of Turkish mounted pistols. At this moment he was half resting on his naked sword with the right hand, while the left was raised with the palm outward, as a sign of peace to the contending parties. He was, indeed, a noble figure as he stood thus before them, so beautiful in person, and so commanding in manner.

CHAPTER II.

"The fight was o'er; the flashing thro' the gloom,
Which robes the cannon as he wings a tomb,
Had ceased; and sulphury vapours, upward driven,
Had left the earth, and but polluted heaven:
The rattling roar which rang in every volley
Had left the echoes to their melancholy;
No more they shrieked their horror, boom for boom;
The strife was done, the vanquished had their doom!"

SINKING THE PRIZE.——THE GOLDEN VALLEY, AND THE ROVER'S STRONGHOLD.—— MODE OF DEMANDING RANSOM.——THE BARBED ARROW.——THE FREEBOOTERS AT PLAY.——THE FIERCE QUARREL, AND ITS PROMPT SUPPRESSION BY THE CAPTAIN. ——THE MUTINEER, AND HIS ATTEMPT UPON RODERICK'S LIFE.——HIS PUNISH- MENT.——THE IMPORTANT SERVICE OF A YOUNG SPANISH PRISONER, WHO SAVED THE ROVER'S LIFE.——DESCRIPTION OF THE YOUNG SPANISH CAVALIER.

A COUPLE of busy hours served to strip the Spanish ship of all that was valuable to the rovers, when she was deliberately scuttled, and the survivors of her crew taken on board the tri-masted schooner, and placed under confinement. After standing off and on by the spot until the galleon had disappeared below the surface of the gulf, the rover lay his course for the mouth of the river that watered the Golden Valley, as they called their retreat.

This name was very appropriate, not only on account of the great wealth that the freebooters had accumulated there, but also for the richness of its tropical fruits that constantly ripened there. The delicious-flavoured rose apple made fragrant the air, mingling its sweetness with the wild heliotrope, and the budding flowers that form the constant ornament of the island. The rich and nutritious banana, the sapota, the cocoa-nut, and all the delicious fruits indigenous to the island and the climate, flourished in rank luxuriance, supplying an agreeable and delightful nutriment for the wild and fearless spirits that inhabited the Golden Valley.

Such was the contrast between the home of the rovers and the fearful deeds that employed them. The soft, delicious climate of Cuba rendered the spot, so beautiful in other respects, but little less than a fairy Paradise. But these charms, so liberally bestowed by nature, seemed to have no influence over the inhabitants of the spot; for though they were under complete subjection to the will of Rode- rick, their chief, who was in years far their junior, still they were a band of fear- ful spirits, that would seem naturally to seek some bleak and barren field for their deeds.

Roderick himself could not have passed more than twenty-three years, but there was that in his calm and collected demeanour, his perfect contempt of danger, and his mode of governing the fiery spirits that surrounded him, that showed, though his years had been few, yet they had been crowded with expe- rience, and must have been passed in the school of trials and danger to have made him what he was. One had only to look deep into his eyes to read much of him; they were remarkable—so belying, in their deep, earnest, and truthful expression, the wild life he pursued. They told at once of a soul within that only needed the occasion to bring out its excellence and worth, in spite of his apparent cruelty of character.

It was the practice of the rovers, after stripping their enemies of all they possessed, to retain them prisoners, exacting liberal ransom from their friends, whom they took good care should be early informed of their capture. Thus with the crew of the galleon just taken by the rovers,—her crew were confined in the Golden Valley, all save one or two passengers, who had been permitted to roam at large, after giving their word of honour as to the manner in which they would improve this liberty. It might have been the third or fourth day subsequent to the capture of the Spanish galleon, when the Barbed Arrow—for so the rovers called their beautiful craft—was lying calmly at anchor, near the shore, in the Golden Valley. The really comfortable homes of the buccaniers made quite a village, there being some thirty of them, dotting the scenery here and there in the most picturesque style. The commander's stood a little apart from the rest, and was also distinguished by the small pennant that floated from its top, a flag with a broad red field. It was a time of rest with the inhabitants of the valley, and they had been amusing themselves at some game, similar to that known in these more modern times as cricket, being played then as now with bat and ball. The players were divided into two equal parties, and each one, as usual, matched against the other. The game had gone on quietly, and in good spirit for some hours, when, on summing up the winnings and losses of each party, a warm dispute arose about some trifle, which soon began to assume a most serious aspect. Men who had no laws or tribunals to fear, save those raised and sustained by themselves at will, were not accustomed to place much restraint upon their passions or actions, and thus gave way at once to a spirit of boyish quarrel that seemed to tempt them.

Roderick had been watching the game for some time with apparent pleasure, but now with eyes upon the ground, and his back placed against the body of a fallen tree, he seemed to be lost in meditation. Already had the two parties of players proceeded to open violence, from words to blows, and even knives were drawn, before their fierce altercation aroused the rover captain from his dream of deep forgetfulness. But the fierce din at last reached his ears, when he suddenly raised his head, and turned towards the conflicting crew. A single comprehensive glance, and he understood the state of affairs at once; a few steps brought him to their very midst. He did not hasten, but merely walked among them, with a calm, determined brow, such as they had ever seen him wear in battle, with the same spirit flashing from his eye. A pistol was in his hand, and he seemed to be singling out the greatest culprit, that he might make an example for the rest. Every one of those fierce spirits were calmed in an instant; not an eye in that desperate crew but sought the ground, abashed at the condition in which their young commander had detected them. It was a strange and wild picture, that in the Golden Valley at this time. There were some thirty or forty of the freebooters, who had been engaged at the game of ball, divided, as we have said, into two equal parties; these had fallen back, each of them, on the near approach of the rover; and he now stood with his light yet noble form between them, and the men quailed before his single glance and arm like so many children. He looked thus upon them for a moment, with a spirit of bitter scorn wreathing his handsome face, and then, after this singular pause, said,—

"Mutiny, rank, open rebellion! Which of you will look me in the eye, that I may know him most to blame, and make him pay the forfeit for the rest of you? And you who have knives, look to it that you do not cut your fingers!"—a dozen were sheathed in an instant!—"Remember, by our contract and your solemn oaths, that no weapons are to be drawn, save by my orders. Pierre Lancellette, that knife is still in your hand," he continued, addressing one of the crew, who had failed to follow the example of the rest, and sheathe his knife. The rover paused for a moment, that the man might improve the hint, but to no purpose, for he seemed determined not to obey, evincing a dogged spirit of wilfulness; though he had not the courage to meet his commander's eye, he muttered some incoherent words half aloud, of a mutinous character, the sound alone reaching his captain's ears.

We say the rover paused, but it was only for a moment, when the ominous click of the lock of his pistol seemed to awaken the disobedient man to his senses. He knew the prompt decision of his captain—he had seen evidences of it before that hour; he knew that he would take his life upon the spot, if he should evince another sign of disobedience, and, therefore, he sullenly placed the knife in his bosom, and turned slowly from the spot, but with a black spirit overshadowing his countenance.

"Now disperse," said Roderick, sternly, to his men; "and do not come together in numbers until you can behave like men."

The men sought their several homes like those who felt the rebuke, were abashed, and would profit by it. Roderick then strolled along the river's bank by himself, without seeming to give the late affair a second thought. He had thus passed beyond the farthest thatched cottage of the group, and entered a little orange grove, pausing to inhale the rich fragrance of the blossoms around him. No one can realise the delightful fragrance of a grove of these trees who has not sauntered among them in their native soil. The rover had passed but a few steps within the clump of trees, when he suddenly heard a pistol discharged so near his ear as to stun him for an instant, but turning promptly, and at the same time grasping a pistol from his own belt, he sought the cause of this singular occurrence. The sight that met his eye was a strange one—he beheld Pierre Lancellette drawing a pistol from his bosom with his left hand, while his right was held aloft, containing the lately discharged weapon, by the grasp of a young man, whom he instantly recognised as one of the prisoners taken in the galleon. The rover sprang with the agility of an animal upon the person of Pierre Lancellette, and with the exertion of a part only of his remarkable strength, wrenched the second pistol from the grasp of the freebooter, and confronted him with his peculiar determined look. The man stood abashed and conquered before him, without daring to lift his eyes from the ground. It was sufficiently evident, without the exchange of a single word, that he had intended to take the life of his captain, and also that this would, in all probability, have been accomplished, had not the young Spaniard opportunely discovered the freebooter in the very act, and, by promptly knocking up his weapon, broke his aim. The rover looked upon him for a moment, during which it was evident that a series of contending emotions moved his breast, so very expressive was his fine, open countenance during the pause. At length, he seemed to have resolved something in his mind, and letting go his hold of the man, he said,—

"Pierre!"

"Captain."

"You have forfeited your life!"

"I know it," said the man, in a subdued tone of voice.

"By our laws, I am your judge and executioner, both."

"It is the law."

"Pierre," said the rover, in an altered tone of voice, which caused the fierce freebooter to start at its very gentleness; "you have never failed me in battle; we have fought side by side, and I know you are brave at heart. Why, then, this cowardly act? Is it the part of a man?"

The culprit made no answer, but half-averted his face.

"Have you had time to cool your brain, Pierre?" continued the rover.

"I have, captain," answered the man.

"I will have no man about me that I cannot trust!"

"I am content," said Pierre Lancellette, believing his last hour had come.

"Pierre!"

"Captain."

"If this attempt had been made against the humblest of our crew, your body should have slept this night beneath the soil of the Golden Valley. Do you hear me, sir?"

"I do, captain."

"As it is, you have only attempted to take the life of your captain, and I forgive you!   Here, sir, is your weapon—it is loaded!"

"Captain!"

"Not a word, Pierre. I like actions better. Go, sir, and though the world calls us buccaniers, let us remember we are men."

The abashed freebooter went his way still deeper into the grove, to meditate upon the late occurrence, and his captain turned his steps with the young Spaniard, to whom he was so much indebted, to his dwelling.

"I owe you my life, signor," said Roderick to his prisoner, as they walked along the river's course together.

"Then I have requited the debt that I owed you," was the reply.

"Debt?" said the rover, inquiringly; "surely you can owe me little, save ill will, for by me you are detained prisoner."

"Do you not remember striking down a spear-point, and reproaching him who held it for attacking an unarmed person?"

"On the deck of the galleon?" asked Roderick, recalling the scene.

"Yes, just before the close of the fight."

"I believe I do remember the scene you refer to," replied Roderick.

"It was I whom you saved, and chance has thus enabled me to repay you the debt in this fortunate manner."

Roderick was deeply interested in the young man, and listened with pleasure to his musical voice. Although of Spanish birth, he spoke French and English, the languages the rovers most employed, almost as well as a native of either country. In years, he could not have been more than sixteen; for, spite of his graceful and noble bearing, there was a slight degree of diffidence about his manner, that showed he lacked the experience of the world that early matures a Spanish cavalier.

"Let us be friends," said Roderick, holding out his hand to the young Spaniard, "if you can feel thus to one like me. From this hour you are free, and the first opportunity shall be improved to forward you on your destination, with a remuneration for your loss."

The Spaniard made no reply, but pressed the rover's hand warmly.

CHAPTER III.

" O'er the glad waters of the dark blue sea,
Our thoughts are boundless, and our souls as free,
Far as the breeze can bear, the billows foam,
Survey our empire, and behold our home !
These are our realms, no limits to their sway,
Our flag the sceptre all who meet obey ;
Ours the wild life in tumult still to range
From toil to rest, and joy in every change.

A SKETCH OF THE BUCCANIERS OF AMERICA.—THEIR WILD AND FEARFUL PRO-FESSION.—ITS CAUSE AND ORIGIN.—THE PECULIAR MODE OF WARFARE ADOPTED BY THEM.—SYMPATHY FOR THE ROVERS BY EUROPEAN NATIONS.—THEIR ASSIS-TANCE GRANTED.—LETTERS OF MARQUE GIVEN.—THE DRESS AND MANNERS OF THE PIRATES.—ADAPTATION OF THE WEST INDIAN ISLES FOR PIRATICAL PUR-POSES.—SKETCH OF A NOTORIOUS PIRATE'S LIFE.

THOUGH it may at first seem strange that a band of freebooters could thus make their stronghold so publicly and boldly in the Spanish possessions of the West Indies, yet when the date of the time is duly considered, the reader will no longer wonder that Roderick and his band could live in comparative safety in the Golden

Valley.   Let us tell you a little of these days and their belongings, sketch you a few items which we have gathered on the spot, with historical correctness, touching the date and locale of our tale.   It is a well authenticated fact, that the iron rule of the Spaniards in America, or rather the West Indian Isles, was the primary cause and origin of that far-famed association, the buccaniers of America.   They sprang up at first from among a class of adventurers, who had sought this region,

HE BEHELD PIERRE DRAWING A PISTOL FROM HIS BOSOM WITH HIS LEFT HAND, WHILE HIS RIGHT WAS HELD ALOFT, CONTAINING THE LATELY DISCHARGED WEAPON, BY THE GRASP OF A YOUNG MAN, WHOM HE INSTANTLY RECOGNISED AS ONE OF THE PRISONERS TAKEN IN THE GALLEON.

partly for the purpose of honest trade, and partly lured hither by the glowing stories that reached the continent of Europe, of the delightful climate and native richness of the islands that form the American Archipelago.   These men, composed mainly of English and French, being at last driven to the utmost extremity by the outrageous oppression of the Spaniards, who claimed sole and entire rule in the islands, whether in present occupation or not, at last took up arms against their vindictive and bloody enemy, and being few in numbers, they were compelled to be constantly on the alert, lest they should be surprised and captured by their vigilant foe, who hunted them from spot to spot, and from island to island, like wild animals. The trade of war being thus forced upon them, they soon became inured to its hardships, and being composed of daring and adventurous spirits, they shortly came to look upon this employment as their fixed occupation, and forming themselves into companies, they bound themselves, by the most fearful and profane oaths, to sustain each other to the last drop of their blood, and to prosecute, in every possible manner, their common enemy, the Spaniards, to their last breath. Thus bound and influenced, they gave up all culture of the soil, which with hunting had heretofore been their chief employment, and starting at first in mere boats to sea, they boldly attacked their enemies, and vanquished them with the most awkward materials by their daring and impetuous courage. Thus they performed in a most incredibly short period of time, a series of renowned and brilliant acts against the Spaniards, that history records as unparalleled; and in six months from the first regular formation of their society, they were enabled to take the sea with a fleet of well-found and completely manned ships!

At first, the depredations of the buccaniers were confined solely to the Spanish commerce and settlements in the islands, and on the coast of the main land. Cities were taken and sacked, ransoms demanded, and even regular contributions of black mail were successfully levied upon many ports, the inhabitants being but too happy thus to purchase the protection which they had found, by sad experience, their government or their own arms could not afford them. The occupation and avowed purpose of the buccaniers was not of a character to engender any feelings of honour or true chivalry, but rather to foster the passions of revenge and cupidity, for their constantly increasing gains were positively enormous. The news of their success reached the various ports of England and France, and they were soon joined by others, if possible more reckless and daring than themselves, until their ranks were swelled to large numbers, and their strength became of the most formidable character. Thus emboldened, they grew more and more hardened, and though their main object and purpose remained the same, viz., that of the utter extermination of the Spaniards in America, still they did not hesitate to make prizes of any valuable cargoes that might fall in their way, under whatever flag they chanced to sail, and indeed soon began to scour the seas, with booty alone for their rallying cry.

In Europe generally, the buccaniers were looked upon as merely an association of wild men, or an assembly of robbers of various nations, so far off as not to interfere in the national interests, and therefore best let alone. Indeed, it is well known, that at one time, it was the policy of France and England, and even Portugal and Holland, to secretly aid the buccaniers, which they did by secret contributions of arms, ammunition, and naval stores, and by selling them ships well built, and calculated expressly for their service, in hopes by this means to weaken the power of Spain, upon whom all the rest of Europe looked with a jealous eye. In furtherance of this cunning purpose, during the time of war, which was constantly occurring between Spain and one or the other of these powers, letters of marque were freely granted to the buccaniers, which were employed with good intrepidity and success against the Spanish commerce. It was a novel thing to fight under the semblance of legality, and the rovers took to the thing as quite a joke, though to the enemy they made it a very serious affair. Even after peace was ratified, the buccaniers heeded it not, but still sailed ostensibly under the sanction and protection of their letters of marque—an easy cloak, which, however, they soon wore threadbare.

The dresses of these men forms a singular evidence of their characters. Though possessed of hoards of gold, they seemed to indulge no taste for finery or display of any kind; each buccanier wore a shirt and pantaloons made of coarse linen cloth, dyed red, generally, with the blood of animals. They wore boots of hog skin, without hose, and their heads were covered with a close skull cap of tanned leather, impervious to a spear thrust or sword cut. A strip of raw hide served them for a girdle, and also as a support for a brace or two of pistols, a short heavy sword, well calculated for a hand to hand contest, which was their almost universal mode, and generally one or more knives, and a short broad dagger. Thus equipped and armed with their firelocks, each of which carried a brace of ounce balls, they were emphatically a formidable enemy, and might be said to be armed to the teeth. Among some old and curious state papers in the government house of Havana, there are preserved several paintings, rough to be sure, but well designed, giving a good idea of the real buccanier in full costume.

There is, perhaps, no other section of the globe so well calculated for the purposes of piracy as were the West Indian isles in those days. The innumerable natural havens, gulfs, and small islands, which, though uninhabited, yet abounded with provisions and fruits of all kinds known in the tropics, and especially in fish, tortoises, marine birds, and excellent water. These islands were very easy of access for small embarkations, but could not be approached without most imminent risk by ships or large vessels of any class. The buccaniers improved all these advantages to the utmost; and by cunning, and the most headlong display of courage, exposure to every kind of danger, they accomplished seeming impossibilities, and amassed immense fortunes, which many, however, falling in battle, never lived to enjoy. Stories are told to this day among the islands, of buried treasures discovered, that the freebooters had hoarded by their fearful and bloody deeds.

As in all other associations of men, for whatever purpose, there were scheming and designing ones among the buccaniers, who, often managing to fleece their companions of nearly all they had, gently slipped away to England and settled, expending the enormous amount of gold they had stolen from thieves with a liberal hand.

Such men were always received into good society, and courted for their great wealth and liberality; and we may one day take occasion to write out the history of one of this class, a sort of piratical nabob, whose family drive their coach in the streets of London at this writing. The parent himself has long since gone to his long home, but the money that supports that aristocratic family was once buried beneath the soil of the Tortugas by pirates. In the meantime, and in illustration of our story, let us tell you, in a few word, of the life of one of these buccanier leaders of the West Indies.

The early part of the seventeenth century was memorable for the bloody deeds of the freebooters; stories of their daring and successful fights rang from one end of Europe to the other—tales of the utmost seeming extravagance were told of their prowess, and disbelieved while they were yet true, but still nothing could deter the avaricious Spaniards from sending their ships into these seas, lured hither by the riches of Mexico and Peru, for when a successful voyage was consummated, it made the fortunes of all concerned for life. One of these fine Spanish galleons, well found in every belonging, not forgetting that of a full armament, was standing round the extremity of Cape Filburon, on the west coast of the island of St. Domingo, one mild tropical evening, the sun was just setting, and the golden sky was throwing most glorious hues athwart the ship's course upon the rippling waters. There was scarcely any motion to the vessel, so lightly did the gentle trade wind fan the sails,—ah! those refreshing trade winds in the tropics—no one was on deck save the drowsy helmsman, and a few men who were sleeping on the deck forward. The officers were playing cards in the cabin, and there was an appearance of comfort and safety about the vessel, that looked truly inviting as she rose and fell on the easy motion of the swelling sea, just parting the blue waters at her bow, as she gained steerage way on her leisurely course.

Suddenly a new figure bursts upon this quiet scene. A small boat, with a single sail, shoots out from the projecting point of the cape. It is a mere cockle shell of a boat, and is crowded to overflowing by the twenty men it contains. It is steered directly for the unconscious Spanish vessel, and being light, the wind soon puffs her to the side of the galleon, aided by the oars of her crew. So quietly have they approached the vessel, that even the drowsy helmsman has not taken the alarm, barely opening his eyes now and then to see that he has his course by compass, then drops into a state of forgetfulness again. Those in the boat clamber to the side of the Spanish vessel, bore a hole in the bottom of their little boat, and as she sinks along side, spring altogether upon the deck. The attack is sudden, it is desperate—it is by the pirates! Fierce is the conflict; the rovers despatch every one that opposes them, and out of the two hundred men that make the crew of the vessel, more than ninety lie dead upon the decks! The remainder of the crew surprised, and trembling at the fearful character of their enemies, surrender. Not having observed the buccaniers when they approached the galleon, and seeing no vessel now in sight, the suspicious Spaniards declared them to be devils fallen from the sky! Thus was the victory easily won by the pirates, who lost but four of their number in the desperate encounter with the foe, whom they had completely surprised.

The survivors of the Spanish crew were landed on the nearest island, and left to take care of themselves, all save a few who were retained to manage and work the vessel.

When the buccaniers examined their prize, they found that they had conquered one of immense value, enough, if equally shared, to afford an ample fortune to each and every one of them. A consultation was immediately holden, and the commander and his followers decided to leave for ever their present mode of life, return to Europe, and settle down for the future, where they might end their days without further strife or risk. Determined to run no risk of losing the great prize they had now possessed themselves of, they resolved to leave that which they had buried on the island, and sail directly across the ocean, never again to return to those scenes which they had rendered so memorable by their deeds of blood and cruelty.

The ship arrived safe in France, her cargo was advantageously disposed of, and her crew, or rather that portion of it who were masters, each received a princely fortune as his share. They then separated, some settling in the environs of Paris, some in England, and one or two boldly taking their way to Spain, choosing that country for a home!

The captain of this wonderfully successful crew of buccaniers was the renowned Pierre le Grand, who for a series of years was a captain among the freebooters, and who was possessed of so implacable a hatred against the Spaniards, that it is said he never spared the life of a fighting Spanish man who was once in his power, until the instance of this remarkable and last capture. He declared that he had fully glutted his revenge, and that he was tired of playing the executioner any longer.

A few such heavy losses as this last awoke the king of Spain, and made him realise that the freebooters must be exterminated from the West Indies, at all hazards, cost what it might, or else he would be forced to withdraw all title to dominion in these waters. A whole fleet of vessels was, therefore, fitted, and sent out to accomplish this purpose, in which, however, they but partially succeeded. Spain herself would never have been able completely to exterminate the buccaniers, for it was not until England, France, and even the United States, as late as the beginning of the eighteenth century, joined in the purpose, and they may be said to have disappeared. And even since that period, the gulf has more than once been the scene of piratical deeds, as the records of Lafitte will show.

Our hero was not one of that band; and though the world could hardly make the distinction, yet was he actuated by an entirely different spirit from what animated them.

CHAPTER IV.

> "Such were the notes that from the pirate's isle
> Around the kindling watch-fire rang the while;
> Such were the sounds that thrilled the rocks along,
> And unto ears as rugged seemed a song !
> In scattered groups upon the golden sand,
> They game, carouse, converse, or whet the brand;
> Select the arms, to each his blade assign,
> And careless eye the blood that dims its shrine."

THE ROVER AND HIS PRISONER.—CAVALIER'S HISTORY.—MOTIVE OF RODERICK.—HIS CONNECTION WITH THE BUCCANIERS.—ANTICIPATED PRIZE.—DECISION OF A PRISONER.—SIGNAL FROM THE LOOKOUT.—THE BARBED ARROW FLIES AWAY TO SEA.—ROVER'S CREW, AND CHARACTERS THAT COMPOSE IT.

Soon after the first meeting between the rover and the young Spaniard, they became warm friends; for there was a strange degree of chivalry and honour mixed up in the character of Roderick, that somehow seemed to touch an answering chord in the bosom of his prisoner. There seemed to be a certain unity of feeling between them, that we sometimes experience between ourselves and another, though we may have been strangers until the hour that we realise the truth of this. Good apartments were supplied for all the Spaniards, but one in his own cottage was allotted to the youthful cavalier, which threw them, from necessity, still more together. They strolled together over the beautiful valley and its environs, exchanging the emotions of their hearts, and cementing thereby a feeling of warm friendship. They were reclining, after a short walk, on the banks of the river that watered the Golden Valley, one soft afternoon in June, when the conversation turned upon each other's history. The Spaniard mentioned the subject first, hoping to draw Roderick out; but the rover adroitly turned the application, so that his companion was forced to answer by his own history, which he did after some hesitancy, as follows, telling his story in a low and sweetly musical voice, in pure English.

"I was born in the suburbs of Madrid, in Spain, in our family mansion, an old style castle or fortress, the foundation of which must have been laid as far back as the middle of the fifteenth century. My father, a proud and wealthy Castilian of pure blood, kept regal state in our halls, and more than three score of gallant cavaliers, well skilled in war, sat at his table as retainers. Ah! my home was a happy one, captain. I was an only child, and every care was lavished upon me that the fondness of a dear mother could suggest, or the experience of a father procure. My father's wealth, birth, and the stronghold he occupied, all served to render him one whom his sovereign was anxious to number among his friends, and therefore my parent was a favoured man at court, sharing the advice and confidence of his sovereign.

" I need not tell you of the unhappy divisions and civil wars that have so long been the curse of my poor country; these you must already be familiar with. My father strenuously avoided all connection with either of the great contending parties, though at heart he was scrupulously loyal, never hesitating to express himself to this effect upon all fitting occasions. But the king deemed all those who did not join actively with him in the favourite political measures of the crown, were in reality against him; and reasoning on this wise, his sovereign, on the breaking out of the last civil war, looked upon our house with a suspicious eye. The faithful deeds of a long line of loyal ancestors were all overlooked, my father condemned unheard by the king, and in the excitement of the times, by a cunning trick was lured from the castle, and by stratagem made prisoner to the king's

troops. A mock ceremony in form of a trial was at length procured, and he was condemned as a traitor, his life declared forfeited, and his estates confiscated. No heed was taken of the host of evidence offered in his behalf by the king or his ministers; he was readily condemned and beheaded—the same edict which declared the sentence also stating that his family must leave the country as continual exiles.

"Every branch of our family had fallen equally under the ban of the throne, and thus forsaken, it was determined that we should seek my mother's brother, now residing somewhere in the West Indies. For this purpose, we took passage in the vessel you captured for these seas; but, alas! the grief that beset my mother's heart wore fast and fatally upon her, and before we had been three weeks at sea, she was buried beneath the waves! I need not attempt to describe to you my feelings. I see you pity me."

"I do, indeed, poor boy," said the rover, encouragingly.

"Well, time passed on, and at length we met you on the waters. I cannot say whether I was sorry or glad to do so, for a spirit of recklessness had taken complete possession of me, that led me to hail any change as desirable. I looked upon the bloody fight that ensued with a calm indifference that surprised even myself. I did not even take a weapon in my hand, but awaited the decision of the battle with calmness. You gallantly saved my life just at the close of the contest, by striking off the spear-head that one of your followers had aimed at my heart. From that hour to the present you know my hourly occupations."

All this was told with an earnest truthfulness of style, yet in a vein so gentle, and in a voice so sweet, as to charm the rover, who had listened throughout with the greatest interest and attention to the words of the young cavalier, whose full, dark, and expressive black eye was bent upon him the while.

"Believe me," said Roderick, "I sympathise truly with you, and freely offer you any aid in my power."

"Such words of kind assurance we meet where least expected," said the young Spaniard; "who would have sought it in my instance here in the West Indian isles—and shall I say it?—at the hands of a freebooter!"

"The name is perhaps merited," said Roderick, thoughtfully; "or at least in part; and yet I have never made a prize of any other than a Spanish vessel, against which nation I declare open war."

"And from what motive do you persecute the commerce of Spain?"

"For plunder, of course," said Roderick, with a forced smile.

"Not so," said his companion; "I have been with you long enough to read your character better, far better than to believe this."

The rover started, and looked thoughtfully at his companion for a moment, and said,—

"I will tell you, Signor Mattenez,"—so the young man had signed his name on the list of prisoners—"for I do feel a singular desire to have your good-will and respect,—matters that I have thought little of lately, save that I have tried to keep still my own conscience. I have hardly an incentive to virtue or honour. Circumstances which would be of little interest to you drove me from my native land. I sought to find some spot where the stirring character of the time might lead me for a time to forget myself; and perhaps actuated, also, in some degree by a feeling of cupidity."

"Not for the sake of gold," interrupted the Spaniard, keenly; "but for something that it would bring."

"Be that as it may," continued the rover, "I knew the belongings of a ship from a mere boy, and early learned to manage one. The sea appeared to be a fine field for exertion. Stories were constantly reaching England of the black injustice of Spain to all settlers in these islands, of her unfeeling oppression, and even bloodthirsty conduct towards them, until in self-defence these would-be peaceable settlers were driven to adopt the profession of arms, both for self-protection, and as an employment to support themselves, having thus been deprived of all other means of a livelihood. They gained much sympathy in England. I determined to join them as the weaker party, and to fight against the Spaniards. I came hither and united with the buccaniers; but I found no congenial spirits among them, and indeed was not prepared in my own mind to go to such lengths as they did in the prosecution of their designs; so we separated, and I assumed a separate command, to carry out the spirit of my original purpose; and I believe I have in no instance departed from the honourable and acknowledged rule of warfare, as established and recognised between nations."

"Then I do wrong to call you a freebooter," said the Spaniard; "perhaps if I bore my king much love, I should be less inclined to look so leniently upon your profession; but I can no longer entertain feelings of loyalty towards a king who has taken the life of one parent, and caused the decease of another. Would that all the internal enemies of Spain were actuated by as honest motives as yourself."

"I have sure intelligence of the coming upon the coast of a richly laden ship within a few days," said Roderick; "indeed we look hourly for her appearance. I must possess her wealth, but for your sake the vessel shall be spared, that you may thus be enabled to go on your way to meet the uncle of whom you spoke."

The Spaniard looked thoughtfully upon the ground for a moment, and then turning to the rover, said,—

"I have no desire to quit the Golden Valley, unless my company is already irksome to its master."

"Indeed!" said the rover, not a little surprised; then continuing, "I shall feel a blank in my heart when you are gone. But do you mean that you would be contented here, with the rude associations of the place?"

"Most certainly, I do! I have never seen my uncle. I do not know his character; and as to the people who surround him, they would know me as one who had been banished from my country and home, and treat me, perhaps, accordingly. For these reasons, and as I cannot return to Spain, I had rather stay here, assured as I am of your friendship."

"So long as you feel thus," said the rover, "you are welcome to share the friendship, cottage, and cabin of Roderick."

A singular unanimity of feeling had sprung up between these two; one, fresh from the hot-bed of Spanish aristocracy; the other leading the life of a buccanier. Have you not, as we have before asked, sometimes met with one whose soul seemed to be moulded similar to your own—one in whom you could see every prompting of your own, reflected as in a mirror, or who could sympathise in the peculiar feelings that you had so often tried in vain to explain to others? Just so it was with Roderick and the young Spaniard,—they seemed like brothers, and in the society of each other appeared to have found a new world.

Just as Signor Mattenez was warmly thanking Roderick for his offer, the report of a pistol shot reached their ears from the look-out on a neighbouring eminence. It was the signal of a sail in sight!

"Do you choose to remain here?" asked the rover; "or shall I detain the vessel he has just signalised for your purpose?"

"I will remain," said the Spaniard, placing his hand within the rover's.

The Barbed Arrow slipped her moorings, and dropped quietly down the river, with all her crew on board, spreading sail after sail the while, so that when she opened into the gulf, she looked, as she bore away to sea, like a white sea gull just rising from the marshes in its flight off shore. The crew, as we have said, were all on board, and every token of prompt discipline was apparent, while the beautiful fabric "walked the waters like a thing of life." The enemy soon hove full in sight, proving to be a Spanish galleon of heavy tonnage, and apparently well-manned, for her sails were promptly laid aback, while she paused on her course to examine the schooner's movements. In the meantime the rovers fast neared their enemy. The young Spaniard had asked permission to accompany the expedition; it was freely granted, and he now stood by Roderick's side, on the quarter-deck. The freebooters were under arms, and as they stood quietly by their guns, the rover remarked to his companion upon their various characters.

"Yonder short, thick-set man with the pipe is a Dutchman; you see his arms are folded. He goes into battle with perfect resignation, thinking if it is fore-ordained that a bullet shall reach his heart, it will do so, and there's no use in worrying about it; he has a deal of courage, and is a man to rely upon. That smiling fellow by his side is a Frenchman, and I warrant me is cracking some joke upon the Spanish fellow yonder; he would have his laugh out, if a ball were to take off one of his limbs. He is a fine hand to have on board to keep good humour afloat. That thick-set, burly-looking fellow on the larboard bow, there at the gun, is an Englishman—you see how he eyes the enemy. I would lay a wager that he is calculating now, how many good sound blows he will get a chance to give the enemy. He belongs to a dogged race who have courage like an animal, and about as much discretion; he would board that ship alone, if I would let him, and fight till he died. There's a couple of Irishmen at that long-Tom, men who work well in action, and with a good will—knocking an enemy on the head while they breathe a prayer for his soul! Pierre, you see there, is the captain of that gun, and you will see directly with what precision he will use it. It was a little selfish in me the other day to spare that fellow's life in the orange grove, for I could hardly afford to lose him. That negro by the starboard after gun, is a strange being; he is as affectionate to those who use him well as a fellow can well be. He has a strange way of fighting, and I would have you mark him. When we have got fairly at it, he throws away his pike and sword, and springing into the midst of the hand to hand fight, with bare arms, he dashes those enormous fists of his into the face and eyes of the enemy, until he pounds many of them to death! He laughs at sabre cuts and knife stabs. I have seen him covered with them from head to foot, after a hot contest, and yet he would sit down to a hearty meal, and enjoy it! He seems to be made of iron."

"But stay," said the rover, levelling his glass at the Spaniard; "this fellow is getting near enough for a salute; we must be ready for him."

CHAPTER VI.

"Again their own shore rises on the view,
No more polluted with a hostile hue;
No sullen ship lay bristling o'er the foam,
A floating dungeon; all was hope and home.
A thousand vessels darted o'er the bay,
The whitened foam tracking their graceful way.
And peace ruled there about the island shore,
Where honest fishers dipped the pliant oar."

ISLE OF MAN.—ITS HISTORY.—LORD WITHINGHAM'S CASTLE.—TWO SONS.—GRACE MARTIN, THE FISHERMAN'S DAUGHTER.—DESIGN OF LORD CHARLES.—APPOINTMENT.—TEMPTATION.—WHO WAS THE DELIVERER.—WOUND FROM A BROTHER'S HAND.—WHO RODERICK REALLY WAS.

WITH us now, gentle reader, to the Isle of Man. Situated at nearly equidistant from the three principal divisions of Great Britain, it was many years a disputed territory, and held as neutral ground by the different powers, at the time to which we refer, who governed in its vicinity. The only stronghold or rather considerable mansion on the island for some centuries, was that of Lord Withingham's family castle. His ancestors had claimed possession of the island before him, and he himself was born there. His castle was built after the old Moorish style, only remarkable for strength, and a useless expenditure of material in the construction of towers, arches, and nearly innumerable divisions or apartments. The ancient-looking pile was located on one of the eminences of the island, so that from its towers, in fair weather, England, Ireland, and Scotland were all visible. In this castle home dwelt the Withingham family, consisting of the old lord, his lady, and two sons, with some forty or fifty retainers and servants. The environs of the castle had been so laid out and managed, that there were many delightful promen-

"AH, MY GOD! WOULD YOU RUIN A POOR GIRL FOR LIFE?"—*See page* 19.

ades and rides about it. Sporting of all kinds, too, was excellent, and many of the nobility of the neighbouring countries passed weeks at a time with Lord Withingham, gaming and fishing to their heart's content, and sharing freely of the generous bounty of the noble master. Thus his board was rarely without some noble guest, and the castle was a constant scene of gaiety and pleasure, notwithstanding its seemingly secluded and lonely situation.

Lord Withingham was himself a pretty fair specimen of the old English gentleman of the seventeenth century. He was proud, very proud, and sensitive as to his noble birth, which, indeed, was unquestioned; he was a kind, yet in some respects a severe father. His sons were educated alike,—Charles, the elder, was his brother's senior by some four years; and according to the custom of the English aristocracy, was brought up to know that he was expected to sustain in himself the honour and name of the family, while William but too early learned what it was to be a younger brother. Both were allowed every advantage that the times offered for an education; and at the time when we introduce them to the reader, were nearly equal in attainments, William twenty, and Charles twenty-four. There was little to choose between them in personal appearance—they were both fine specimens of the youth of the times. Their near proximity to the sea had led them to pass much time upon the waters, and thus had nature been aided by the invigorating influence of exercise and fresh air, in developing their forms, and in endowing them with those beauties of person attendant upon good health.

In many of the athletic and manly sports that the customs of the day rendered the young men of every class familiar with, the younger brother greatly excelled his elder. On such occasions, a fierce, dark expression suffused the countenance of Charles, but William heeded it not, for he considered that his brother truly loved him at heart, and that such evidence of feeling was but a momentary thought of regret at being excelled; but he knew not the secret promptings of his brother's heart, else he would have seen that he hated him for the superiority of strength and skill that he evinced. Every token of the true state of his feelings towards William was studiously avoided, and none of the family even suspected it, except, indeed, the old steward of the family. He was born on the estate, and had learned to look up to his lord and the young gentlemen as little short of deities; and in his constant attendance upon them, he discovered, to his no small uneasiness, this spirit, but like a faithful servant as he was, he held his peace and said nothing, while in his own humble way, he endeavoured to put everything in such a state as to cause a good spirit to prevail with Charles.

Each successive month seemed to develop more and more this evil spirit in the elder brother, who appeared to think that, fortune having placed him first in birth, he must be first in everything, more especially as he was to be the future heir and representative of his father's noble house. Matters had arrived at this state, when William became exceedingly unhappy from a realising sense of his brother's feelings, and grew thoughtful, excluding himself much from the society of all, and wandering on the sea-shore, or with his gun and dog in the woods. The fine location of the island for the purpose of fisheries had induced several men of this employment to settle not far from the castle, where they pursued their peaceful occupation undisturbed. One of this class, Philip Martin, was the nearest neighbour to the gates of the mansion, and made it a portion of his regular employment to supply the family with the fine fish that abound in the neighbouring waters. After returning from his day's toil, he generally sent in a basket of the best of his fish to the castle by his daughter Grace, a beautiful rustic, as simple as lovely, and as gentle at heart as she was attractive in person. Grace Martin was the very impersonation of rosy health, her lips were full and pouting, her face round and very regular in its profile, her eyes as blue as the sky, and her hair a light auburn, bound always in a modest snood behind and parted plain in front. Grace was not tall, nor short, but just a happy medium. She was born within a pistol shot of the castle, nor had she ever been on the main land. She knew nothing of the natural deceits of the world, and all her experience was gained from a parent whose means of knowledge were of the most limited character. Grace was a great favourite at the castle; every one loved her for her gentle and innocent disposition, and there was always a welcome for her among the domestics of the family. Charles Withingham saw Grace almost daily as she grew up into womanhood; he saw the budding beauty of her person, and coolly marked her for his victim! He always had a kind word for her when they met, and took good care that the price she received for her basket of fish should be more than ample. In this way, by no apparent effort, he won the good-will of Grace's father, and of course, in her simplicity, of Grace herself.

It was strange that Grace, simple as she was, could not see the design of young Lord Withingham. She soon fell into his cunningly laid trap, of meeting him on the sea-shore, and walking in lonely spots. Charles knew very well when to look for her, and so he would happen to be at the gate as she came out, with some gentle word for her ear.

"Well, Grace," he would say, "has your father had good luck upon the fishing-grounds to-day?"

"Pretty good, my lord; not so many as usual, perhaps, but they are very fine ones," she would often reply.

"You are looking remarkably well to-day, Grace; your cheeks put to shame those red roses in your little lattice garden!"

"Do you think my cheeks as red as those roses, my lord?" said Grace, appealing to him in all earnestness.

"Quite, my good Grace, and far more lovely than they."

"You talk so strange, my lord," said the modest girl, blushing as she seemed to realise some inward sense of impropriety.

"Shall you be walking by the shore this evening, Grace?" he asked.

"Certainly, my lord, if you wish it," she replied, unhesitatingly.

"Then we can see how the sea looks by moonlight, Grace. There is no need of any other persons knowing that we are there together, because they might interrupt our conversation. Will you remember this, Grace?"

"Certainly, my lord, I will be on the shore this evening," she replied, pleased in her innocence to think that she could afford pleasure to a lord, by her simple presence, and alone.

Ah, Grace! thy mother has left untaught an important lesson, and we fear that your instructress must be sad experience!

Lord Charles had, by kind words and frequent attentions, such as we have alluded to, brought the sweet girl to the degree of confidence that we have seen her display; and doubtless he believed that he had sufficiently matured his diabolical plan, for this was the first time he had ever made an actual appointment to meet Grace, though he had often managed to do so by seeming chance. They met that evening in secret on the sandy shore; they walked together, and the temptor breathed, in low accents, his tale of deceit and wickedness; he talked of love, and the warm affections of the heart, until he made poor Grace weep, for she believed him sincere. They walked on and on, until they were far from home, and in the skirts of the woods. Lord Charles had drawn Grace's trembling arm within his own, and still whispered his words of deceit in her believing ear, until at last the vileness of his heart was unmasked by a single proposition! Then Grace awoke from the strange spell that had seemed to bind her, and said,—

"Ah, my God! would you ruin a poor girl for life?"

"Nay, Grace, be not so moved; you shall always find a friend in me. It needs not the parson's bans to unite true hearts!"

"My lord, my lord, I pray you let go my waist, have compassion on me; you do but jest, I am sure."

"Nay, but Grace, I assure you I am in earnest—I will always be your friend—you shall want for nothing."

"Will you not unhand me, my lord? Ah! think that from a mere child I have been taught almost to revere your name. I pray you do not give me cause to curse it. My lord, my lord!"

At this moment an arm was thrust between them, the fainting girl was torn from his grasp, and himself cast headlong upon the ground. He staggered to his feet, for the force of the shock had nearly stunned him, and turning, beheld in Grace's deliverer his own brother! Lord William had laid Grace gently upon the green sward, and was already bathing her temples with the cool water hard by. His brother, thus foiled, could not speak for rage, his sword was in his hand in an instant, and the next it had pierced his brother's side, aimed at his heart. William staggered, but with a determined spirit still sustained himself, and endeavoured to revive poor Grace Martin, while his brother, turning from the spot, walked coolly away. A few moments more served fully to revive the fainting girl; and raising her face, she looked about her, bewildered for a moment, then recognising the person of William, who was partially sustaining her form, she seemed to realise that he had protected her, and intuitively laid her head upon his breast. In spite of the painful wound, he had received by his brother's hand, William felt the blood course quickly through his veins as the beautiful girl thus confided in him. It was but for a moment, when Grace, fully recovering herself, sprang to her feet, saying,—

"Ah! my lord, alas, alas, your brother! your brother!" She could say no more, but wept like a child.

William, faint from the loss of blood, could muster just sufficient strength to offer a few consoling words, reassuring and comforting her, when Grace discovered for the first time his wound.

"My God! can it be that he gave you this?" she said, tearing away a portion of her dress to stanch the blood; "and you incurred it for my sake! Ah! my lord, lay your head here," she said, adjusting his person, as he now reclined partly on the ground, and partly in her lap, while she bound up his wound with a portion of her dress. He was severely, but not very dangerously wounded. With Grace's kind assistance, he succeeded in reaching her father's cottage, enjoining upon her a promise of secrecy as to the manner and cause of the wound. Here he managed to remain in secret for a few days, during which time he was enabled to think over and reflect upon his brother's conduct. He did not feel the least prompting of revenge towards Charles; he freely forgave him for the injury he had done him, though in relation to the insult to Grace, he could not but feel indifferently. He could no longer respect him, and he feared also that his own feelings of retaliation might possibly be aroused by some further act of hostility, and be thus led to do that which he might be sorry for.

During his confinement Grace was his constant companion, and necessarily his confidant. He determined to leave his home and the island; he had few ties to make him love home; his parents so palpably favoured his brother in all things, that he could not help constantly realising the slight. To enable him to leave the island, his yacht must be manned; two men he always had on board. Four more were easily secured with provisions, and a sum of money that was at his command. A short letter was left for his brother. He told the latter that he should never reveal the secret that he had chanced to learn, or ever refer to the scar that was on his left side, and that he was parting from him for ever. Grace, the good, dear, grateful girl, arranged all the little matters for his departure with the old butler, who was also necessarily let into the plan of his young master's purpose, first promising to be secret. When at last Lord William Withingham left his home, he pressed a warm kiss upon his nurse's forehead, saying,—

"May God bless you, Grace! Remember me as a brother."

Her heart was too full for utterance. She could only press his hand to her lips and weep. Need we tell the reader that Roderick the Rover and Lord William Withingham are the same?

———

CHAPTER V.

" Alas the moon should never beam,
  To show what man should never see !
I saw a maiden on a stream,
  And fair was she !
And still I stayed a little more,
  Alas! she never comes again ;
I throw my flowers from the shore,
  And watch in vain.

DEPARTURE.——PROPOSALS TO BECOME A SLAVER.——RESOLVES TO JOIN THE BUCCA-
NIERS.——HIS APPRENTICESHIP.——CHANGES HIS NAME.——HIS NAME HEARD OF AT
HOME.——ONE WHO KNOWS HIM.——ENGAGED WITH THE SPANIARDS.——PRIZE.——
PRISONERS FOR RANSOM.——THE SPANISH CAVALIER.——WONDERFUL VISION OF
BEAUTY.

LORD William Withingham, the youngest brother, thus expelled from his home,
spread the sails of his yacht, a swift sailing boat, of some eighty tons burden, and
sailed for Liverpool. This far-famed maritime city was then comparatively but an
infant in growth. Its after rapid rise and final wealth was mainly owing to the
immense profit realised by its merchants in the slave trade, upon the coast of
Africa. Vast numbers of vessels were annually fitted out from this port for the
coast, to engage in this legalised piracy. When William Withingham arrived at
Liverpool, with his trim-built little craft, he was immediately importuned by those
employed in this unholy trade to become an agent in a business, which he was
assured would not only afford ample opportunity for the indulgence of an adventurous disposition, but also to ensure to him within the lapse of a short period of
time an ample fortune.

Almost reckless from a realising sense of his situation in the world, being virtu-
ally banished from home, by the force of circumstances, and also influenced by the
representations of the artful agents set to work upon him, he did for a short time
entertain their proposition, as to engaging in the trade referred to, but when he
came to realize upon the true character of the business, his generous mind revolted,
and he determined to join in some more creditable enterprise. There was at this
very time a vessel fitting out in the harbour of Liverpool, with some degree of
secrecy, destined, as he had learned, for the West India Isles, to join the buccaniers
of those seas against the Spaniards. Lord William talked over the matter with
the captain, a man who had seen service in those waters, and easily satisfied himself as to the aggressive character of the war upon the part of the enemy, and
immediately determined to join the buccaniers as the weaker party, and fight
against the Spaniards, conceiving the so-called freebooters to be in no small degree
in the right. As we have already related, he did join the buccaniers, but soon
learned that they were actuated and moved by too great a spirit of cupidity to
allow them to consider the Spaniards alone as their enemies, and therefore, after a
few months' connection, he left them, and in a beautiful craft that he had ordered
from Liverpool, built expressly for him, and which we have already partially
described to the reader, he now scoured these seas with unprecedented success,
making war on the Spaniards alone. A crew was easily enlisted under his banner,
as he offered regular wages, in addition to the regular division of prize-money,
and in this way he was enabled to choose his men, and to command a picked
crew.

Three years had elapsed from the period at which the younger brother left his
home on the Isle of Man, when we introduced him to the reader. From reasons
of delicacy, which we all can appreciate, he had immediately dropped his family

name on leaving the island of his nativity, assuming that of Roderick Harrol; but after he became notorious as a daring and successful buccanier, he was universally called by the freebooters themselves, and even in different parts of Europe, when his name became well-known, as was the case, Roderick the Rover, and many times had it been inadvertently pronounced around the family hearth, at his home in the castle, accompanied with the relation of well-fought battles against the Spaniards, or of relief freely given to vessels in distress, and particularly those of England, without ever a thought as to whom Roderick really was, much less surmising that it was the lost son of their house. There was one who sometimes heard these stories, and once or twice with a description of the person of the rover, and then she declared within her own heart that she knew who it was, but only to herself. This was Grace Martin, the beautiful daughter of the fisherman. She remembered his strangely important service, and she was not one who could soon forget William Withingham.

The reader will remember that we left Roderick and the Barbed Arrow nearing the Spanish ship off the coast of Cuba. Already had they got within hailing distance, when the Spaniards, knowing full well whom they had to deal with, commenced the engagement by firing a broadside at the rover's craft. Roderick heeded not the first nor second discharge of his enemies' guns, but waited until he was so near upon them that he could distinctly mark out their countenances, when the word was passed quietly forward for the men to stand ready by their guns.

"Pierre," said the rover, addressing the freebooter already referred to.

"Ay, ay, sir," said the man, denoting his attention to his command.

"Is your gun all ready there, with double shot?"

"Ay, ay, sir, loaded and primed, and she will go off of herself if your honour don't give the order before long."

"Give that fellow a shot, Pierre, among the officers on the quarter-deck."

"Just over his larboard quarter, sir?" asked Pierre, preparing.

"That's the spot—blaze away now, with a good aim."

Hardly had the command left the lips of the rover captain, when a shower of splinters flew upon the quarter-deck of the galleon, and the evident consternation that reigned on board showed that more than one life had paid the forfeit for that fearfully accurate discharge. Again and again did the practised rovers plant their iron messengers in the hull of the galleon and among the crew of the Spanish vessel, tacking and sailing in every direction around the enemy, which they were easily enabled to do, from the fact of their own light draught of water, and the cumbersome character of the Spanish galleon. At last, having lost many of his crew, and become much disabled in his running gear, the Spanish captain was forced to lower his flag to the rover! She proved a rich prize to the captors, who took her to the Golden Valley, and after entirely stripping her of all that was valuable to them, it was determined to fill her with the prisoners, and to send her to Porto Bello, where it was known a handsome ransom would be paid for their deliverance. Retaining in their possession the two captains of the prizes last taken, with the first officers, and one or two passengers of some distinction, the rover permitted the vessel to sail with the rest, bearing the message to the authorities, that if a boat was sent, bringing ransom for those already returned and for those retained, then the latter should also be liberated, otherwise their lives should pay the forfeit. This never failed to bring the ransom, and in this case the Spanish vessel lay but a couple of days in the Golden Valley, after which, with a portion of the crew of the former prize, she sailed as a sort of cartel with these orders for Porto Bello.

As we have before taken occasion to show, Roderick and the young Spanish cavalier had become very familiar, and indeed there seemed to be a singular feeling of intimacy existing between them, for they passed much of their time together. The rover was reclining beneath a lofty palm one fine afternoon, overlooking from the rising point he occupied the most beautiful portion of the Valley and the river's course, when the young Spaniard approached the spot, and reclining against the tall palm that shaded the rover, he paused to admire the picture spread out to view in the Golden Valley below them; Roderick turned towards him, and said,—

"Ah! signor, you, too, have come to enjoy the delightful coolness of the sea-breeze from this point. We are many hundred feet above the Valley, and how very beautiful it looks!"

"I have sauntered hither, partly to enjoy this delightful prospect, and partly to meet you, captain," said the Spaniard.

"How knew you that I was here, good Signor Mattenez," asked the rover, somewhat surprised.

"There are good spy glasses in the Valley, captain, and I learned to use one at sea," was the reply.

"You must have a very quick eye to distinguish even with a glass the person of a man from that of a stunted banana," said Roderick, measuring the distance with his eye.

They both paused, and looked with delight upon the glowing scene below them, seeming to be inspired with its gladdening influence. The eye could take in at a glance the entire course of the beautiful river that threaded its course through the valley, and even scan the clear, blue waters of the Mexican gulf beyond.

"Such scenes as these always make me thoughtful, captain," said the Spaniard, "turning, as it were, my eyes in upon my heart, for sympathy. Do you not sometimes feel thus when looking upon such glories as this?"

As the Spaniard spoke, he lifted his outstretched hand and extended it over the scene.

"Yes, signor," sighed Roderick, with a heavy inspiration; "it turns one's thoughts upon home, however distant it may be."

"It is a beautiful theme to dwell upon," added his companion; "it makes us better, captain, and should incite us to well-doing."

Roderick turned his fine expressive countenance upon the speaker.

"Why, is not this a fit time to speak to you as I feel?" he said, after a moment's pause; "since I have first become your prisoner, I have also become your friend; and now feel as deeply concerned for your good, as I could do were you my brother. Ah! Roderick, the noble spirit that actuates you, the fire of your heart should burn to a better purpose, than that which now occupies it. These are no fit associates for such as you, these rough, hardened characters, that form your crew. I know not of your early life, or of the motives that have actuated you in this singular selection of a profession, but I do know that it is not befitting that you should be thus placed in voluntary servitude. Roderick, you were never born for a rover!"

"Signor," said the rover, "until I met you the voice of kind persuasion has been a stranger to my ear for years; little time or inclination have I had to turn back and review my actions, but I have rather sought to forget my troubles in the excitement of governing such spirits as my associates, and in the thrilling pleasure of battle."

"Be persuaded, captain, that this is not your proper sphere," said the noble-hearted Spaniard, earnestly; "resolve to leave it, and join the brilliant circles that you might adorn in civilised life. Why not resolve and act upon this purpose at once?"

"I will think on your words, but press me no further at this time," said Roderick, extending his hand, and pressing that of his companion.

"May the Virgin aid you in your decision," said his companion, as they parted.

"Thanks, thanks," said the rover, turning away by himself.

The rover soon after turned his steps towards the hamlet, and perfected the arrangements for the departure of the rest of his prisoners, the ransom having already been received.

Just at twilight, the long delightful twilight of the tropics, when the golden light of the horizon seems to linger lovingly upon the skirts of the departing day,

Roderick sought the sea-shore alone, after completing the labours of the day. He wandered along the hard gravelly beach, until he came to a spot which was skirted by a growth of trees, when he suddenly paused, and gazed at a sight that was well calculated to entrance him.

Between him and the rich parti-coloured hues of the western sky, he beheld an object bathing in the sea, now floating, and now with a slight exertion shooting forward, and then returning again, and now coming gracefully to land, it rose to the height and form of a beautiful female! Roderick had often heard the strange stories told by the buccaniers of the spirits that haunted these waters, but never before had he made such a discovery as this. His whole frame seemed to be paralysed. The beautiful creature, with a form of the most etherial yet voluptuous loveliness, looked in the uncertain light like a tangible being, so perfect and distinct did it show against the brilliant sky. Never before had Roderick seen a creature that seemed so beautiful. He was too far away to distinguish perfectly the features of the phantom, but the form, the grace, the loveliness! Ah! he was a captive to all; and long after it had disappeared from the shore, he stood there, still gazing upon vacancy, until at length he summoned courage to reach the spot, but the spirit had flown, and no further sign was visible.

It was long past midnight before the rover returned to his couch, and when he did so, it was only to dream of the beautiful spirit he had seen. In his dreams he thought her a sea-nymph, a mermaid, and various were the efforts he seemed to make to reach her, but all in vain. In the morning he rose, fevered and excited, for he was still thinking upon the strange but beautiful spirit. After pressing the hand of his late prisoner, the young cavalier, Roderick urged upon him the importance of departing with the present opportunity, telling him that his words of advice should be treasured, but that his future course was so uncertain that he must urge him to depart.

And thus these two parted warm friends, who had met in battle as enemies.

Time passed on, and the rover daily visited the spot where he had seen the lovely water-spirit, but it came no more. Although the mind of Roderick by degrees assumed its wonted elasticity, still the phantom had made a lasting impression, and in honour of the object of his admiration he named his swift-winged craft, the Spirit of the Wave!

CHAPTER VII.

> " Years had rolled on, and fast they speed away
> To those that wander as to those that stay;
> But lack of tidings from another clime
> Had lent a flagging wing to weary Time.
> They see, they recognise, yet almost deem
> The present dubious, or the past a dream."

ISLE OF MAN.—OLD BEGGAR.—FORTUNE-TELLING.—DISGUISE AND DENOUEMENT. "HE STANDS BEFORE YOU!"—GRACE AND RODERICK.—PAYMENT OF A FINE, AND THE GIFT OF A DOWRY.—LEVI BELT.—MEETING OF TWO BROTHERS.— WOLVES IN SHEEP'S CLOTHING.—BLESSING, KISS, AND PARTING.—SPIRIT OF THE WAVE.

NIGHT was shutting in and around the Isle of Man one mild evening in August, and the last bright rays of the sun were gilding the castle windows of the Withingham mansion, causing them to appear as though they were made of burnished gold, when a poor mendicant knocked at the door and begged for admission, a night's lodging, and food.   The old butler, a kind-hearted man, spoke gently to the poor man, and bade him enter.   He was a wanderer from the main land, who had been carried across by a passing vessel, hoping to find rest and quiet, as he said, from the busy turmoil of the thickly inhabited country, for the poor must know scorn as well as want when among the crowd.   He was a man who had evidently seen much of the world, and who had moved in no inferior class of society.   His form

RODERICK TELLING GRACE'S FORTUNE.

was bent, his hair grey, his voice husky, yet there was the fire of youth in his eye, and the spirit of younger years in his language.   The old butler sat down by his side, and they talked over their experience together.   The strange old man listened with interest to the story of the castle, its early history, and that of the Withingham family.   He was told also of its modern history, of the present Lord Withingham, of his eldest son, and of one who was a wanderer no one knew where.

The night thus passed away in telling these things, and in discussing the excellent cheer prepared by the butler, until it was nearly morning before the two old men retired.

The kind-hearted steward had taken the old man to his own quarters, and bade him make himself at home as long as he chose to tarry, as it was not often that charity was asked on the island, for but few beggars found their way thither. The subsequent morning the old man was up betimes, and started away towards the beach. The cottage of Martin the fisherman lay just in his way, and as he reached its snug and inviting little portal, a sweet voice asked if he would not sit down and rest himself by the door.

"Thanks, gentle maid," replied the old man, to the offer of Grace; "my old limbs weary quickly, and must needs be humoured."

"When were you from the main land, good sir?" she asked.

"Within these four-and-twenty hours. I was at the castle last night."

"Any news from England that can interest us peaceful islanders?"

"I know of none worth the telling, my good girl," replied the beggar.

"What has brought you among us, old man?" asked Grace.

"Partly love of change, partly charity. In my youth I acquired a love of wandering, and still I follow my early bent. I was among gipsies, and this, too, strengthened a natural taste for roaming."

"Were you a gipsy, then?" asked Grace, curiously.

"Something in that way. I learned in those days to tell fortunes; shall I try my power upon you? Let me see your hand."

"If you please," said Grace, with assumed indifference, though her heart beat quick as the old man looked at her palm.

"Let me see," said he, tracing her palm with his finger; "these lines indicate—why, girl, you have already seen adversity in some form, and been rescued from danger and insult. He who would have wronged you was above you in station. Do I not speak correctly?"

"He was, he was," said Grace, much agitated at his words.

"And he who was so fortunate as to render you this service ———"

"Was a younger brother of the man who would have betrayed me," interrupted Grace, with emotion.

"His name was?" The old man paused for an answer, when Grace said,—

"You know all. It was Lord William Withingham!"

"And Grace," said the stranger, calling her by her given name, "he now stands before you!"

As he said this, he cautiously raised an ample wig from his head, and showed the astonished girl the face of Roderick the Rover. Scarcely could she repress a cry of delight, but yet she did heed his signal of caution, and remained mute.

"Can this be possible?" asked Grace, gazing upon him in wonder.

"It is your old friend and playmate that addresses you, Grace."

"Why this disguise—this assumed character?" she asked.

"Because I longed to see my home, the place of my boyhood, my father, mother, and brother. Nay, start not, Grace, at that name. I trust he has given you no further cause for trouble. And then, too, Grace, I wished to see you also," he said, taking her willing hand within his own, while a tear dropped over it from her long eye-lashes. "I could not do this unless disguised, for how could I justify myself to my father without exposing to him Charles's perfidy? You know I have sworn not to do this."

"Would that he had thy noble heart and disposition," said Grace.

"Nay, Grace, you do not know that the world calls me a ———"

"I know," she replied, holding up her hand in caution; "when we have heard of Roderick the Rover—of his helping hand to our vessels in distress—of his many noble acts—of his daring and successful warfare against the bloody Spaniards, others have only thought you a hero—but I knew that it was Lord William Withingham."

"It is indeed singular, Grace, that you should have suspected Roderick and myself to be the same."

"Ah, no," said she, thoughtfully, while her bosom heaved quickly. "I owe everything to you; no wonder, then, that I should have instinctively felt that the hero of a hundred battles was yourself."

"But Grace, how is your friend Levi Belt, of the North side?"

The blush that tinged the before ruddy cheek extended even to her full and beautiful neck, as she answered,—

"He is well, my lord ——"

"Stay, Grace, call me Roderick, if you will, friend, anything but my lord. I entertain none of the feelings of a master towards you. We have been friends from childhood, have grown up as it were together, and by chance we have known a service that has woven still nearer the tie of childhood. Now deal with me, and speak to me, Grace, as though I were your brother, for I have few friends to whom I can speak thus."

"All my service is yours," said Grace; "and I know of nothing that a poor, weak girl might do, that I would not cheerfully attempt to serve you. I know you will believe me, for from infancy the difference in our stations has always been taught me, and I have been brought up to think that no service that either my father, myself, or any other tenant could do for one of the family at the castle, should be held other than a duty and a pleasure. It is both to me."

"Well, Grace, I know your kind heart already—but what of Levi?"

"Ah! he has unfortunately fallen under the ban of your brother. I know not why, unless it be—I am sorry to say—on account of our friendship for each other; but Levi fears him, and is now at sea to escape a threatened imprisonment upon a charge brought against him by your brother Charles, touching an act of trespass upon his grounds."

"Indeed," said Roderick. thoughtfully; "can his evil spirit have so much grown upon him?"

"We were to have been married this month," said Grace, whose eyes again sought the ground; "but Levi was forced away, seemingly in anticipation of this, by Lord Charles."

"Never fear a repetition of this," said Roderick; "what was the form of the complaint?"

"He was accused of poaching upon the land of my lord, and was examined and fined by your father, the justice. He was unable to pay the amount, and rather than be confined, he ran away to sea."

"How much was he fined, Grace?" asked Roderick.

"Five pounds sterling, my ——" She was about to say, my lord, but checking herself, she finished with "friend."

"There are five hundred," said Roderick, placing a purse in her hand heavy with gold and English government bills.

"What am I to do with this?" asked Grace, with some unfeigned tokens of astonishment.

"Pay Levi's fine, and keep the balance for thy wedding dowry, my good girl," replied Roderick.

"Indeed, I cannot take money from you," she said, timidly.

"Nay, Grace, I insist upon it, you have just promised obedience."

"And so heavy a sum," continued Grace, "why, I doubt if my father ever saw so much if all were put together that he has seen from his childhood. Besides, it would impoverish you. Indeed, indeed, but if you could by some means have the fine so arranged that he could be safe, I shall owe you still another important service."

"Do you really think, Grace, that such a paltry sum as that would impoverish me? Why, my poor girl, I am the master of five thousand purses of just its value! I have not fought the dons for nothing, Grace; no, no, they have had to pay pretty roundly for all my services. Take the purse Grace, and remember 'tis thy wedding dowry!"

"I hardly know what to say to your kindness and unbounded generosity, but I have such confidence in your friendship—you are so frank, so noble, so disinterested, that I know you would not counsel me wrong."

"Indeed, I would not, Grace," he replied.

Both now discovered for the first time that some one was approaching them, and was already quite near them. Roderick turned and beheld his brother! He had been cautious and was not off his guard, so that he entertained no fears of discovery, but still talked on to Grace upon some common-place matters, expecting that Lord Charles would pass by when he came to the spot, as the path he now trod passed directly by them. But as he approached the place where they stood, he paused and said,—

"Well, old man, you seem to be making yourself at home—how long do you purpose to remain on the island?"

"I cannot say, your honour," replied Roderick, in his assumed voice, and with a perfect self-control.

"Don't put any nonsense in that girl's head," he continued, frowning upon Grace, who shuddered inwardly at his looks.

"Trust to my discretion, your honour; never fear an old man like me. If the young are to receive instruction at all, from whence can it come so befitting as from old age?"

"Well, well, there are many wolves in sheep's clothing!" Saying this, he turned away, and moodily sought the beach.

"That is very fortunate," whispered Grace, as the elder brother left the spot.

"I do not think that he could disguise himself from me thus, not even time and place helping him."

"Has he ever annoyed you personally, Grace," he continued, after a moment's pause, "since that unhappy evening?"

"Never—he seems to avoid me; but when we do meet, if I chance in making my respect to catch his eye, the expression is fearful."

"His nature is a strange one," said Roderick.

"How will you get away again undiscovered?" asked Grace.

"The same way that I came, Grace. In a secret cove on the north side of the island, my gallant little Spirit of the Wave rides at anchor. I know a secret path hither through the woods, and before the sun sets this night, her anchor will be weighed, and half the course run down the channel to the ocean."

"How much I regret that Levi is not here to thank you for the munificent gift that you have presented to us. Ah! you have done that which will render us independent and comfortable for life with the habits of frugality we have both learned. May God bless you."

"Say no more of it, Grace. I could not serve a sister with warmer satisfaction than I do you."

At this moment the father of Grace made his appearance at the door of the cottage, and as Roderick did not wish to trust his secret to too many heads, he gave Grace a look of intelligence that she understood at once, and pretended to give her his blessing, saying,—

"My blessing upon your gentle head, my good girl," while he kissed her clear high forehead; and the lord and peasant, the fisher-girl and the rover, thus parted from each other.

Roderick knew every path in the dense wood that separated him from his vessel, and taking the most direct, he turned his steps towards the north side of the island, and that afternoon before the sun had set, as her captain had predicted, the Spirit of the Wave was running down the channel with a flowing sail and a graceful air, as if proud of the master spirit that controlled her. Everything about the deck was like clock-work for precision and neatness, and although there were more than a hundred men forming the crew, so well were they drilled and regulated, that each man knew his place, and kept it. There was no confusion or noise on board; all was under the powerful arm of discipline. Even the neatly coiled ropes displayed something of this character, which also pervaded all things. And thus she gaily flaunted like a coquette, as she glided over the sparkling waters of the British channel.

————

CHAPTER VIII.

"Hark! do you hear the look-out cry,
From the lofty shrouds so near the sky?
'A sail! a sail!' he cries;
'She comes from the Indian shore,
And to-night shall be our prize,
With her store of golden ore:
Sail on! sail on!'"

CULLING OUT A CREW.—ENGLISH COAST.—PATRIOTIC RESOLVE.—ROVER'S CABIN. —SUMMONS.—SPEECH.—PREPARING FOR FIGHT.—BATTLE AND VICTORY.— PRIZE.

BEFORE leaving the Golden Valley, on his voyage across the ocean, Roderick had completed a plan which he had long before entertained, that of culling his crew, so as to have only Englishmen under his command. He found that in a heterogeneous combination of national characters, there were ever national themes and questions arising, that kept up a constant undertow of trouble among his men, that required the most watchful care, and prompt discipline to prevent from maturing into actual mutiny. His crew, therefore, now consisted of English, Irish, and a few Scotchmen only—a combination that he found to be the least objectionable for his purpose.

On coming on to the English coast, he learned before he had made the Lizard Point, that a rupture had broken out between England and France, and that the neighbouring waters had already been the scene of several warmly contested naval battles. The thought came over him at once whether he could not serve his country's interests by taking out letters of marque, and entering in this way upon an honourable profession of arms. He had thought seriously on this subject while bound up channel to the Isle of Man, when he visited, as he have seen, the home of his boyhood in disguise.

Actuated by this spirit, he thought seriously of the matter, as a means of carving out for himself a honourable name, and sinking in some degree the remembrance of his former service, which at best wore too lawless an aspect for the contemplation of a sensitive mind. He sat by himself in the cabin of his vessel as she skimmed the waters of the British channel. He had left orders for his officer to steer a south-east course until morning, knowing that by that time he would only be in the neighbourhood of Land's End. Roderick looked like a statue as he sat there so immovable by his cabin table, one arm resting on the table, his limbs crossed and his eyes resting on a stack of pistols and sabres, that were affixed to the opposite side of the cabin in the form of a circle, the points and muzzles inward. An observer would have noticed that though the pupils of the eye rested there, still the mind wandered, and they caused no reflection to the brain of the objects around the cabin.

The profuse richness of the furniture of the cabin bespoke of a lavish disposition, or rather that wealth so lightly held must have been easily obtained. Couches of rich cut velvet surrounded the apartment, and even the partitions dividing the cabin from the run of the between decks, were so covered by hangings of velvet as to look more like easy ottomans, than implements of war. Rare and beautiful paintings, rich gold and silver ornaments, old elaborately wrought mahogany chairs and rich Turkey carpets, told that all parts of the globe had contributed to the furnishing of the rover's cabin. The arrangement of weapons was most admirable, and with the two pieces of ordnance referred to, were such as to enable the occupants in time of mutiny, or of necessity of any kind, to turn the apartment at once into a strong citadel against the crew! All the precautions, too, were visible that would second the authority and power of the master, if necessarily brought in conflict with those under his command, for full well he knew that with such spirits as he was associated with, and in such a service, every precaution should be carefully taken to enable him to maintain his complete and absolute ascendency, which there was no law to back. Immediately under the cabin was the magazine, accessible only through the apartment, thus placing every power within the complete control of the occupant, even to that of being able to blow all to utter destruction in an instant.

The rover had sat thus musing for some time in the apartment we have described, and then rising, he walked the cabin for a few moments, thoughtfully, approaching a hanging gong above his head, he touched it lightly, and a boy opened the cabin door, with a bright, intelligent look.

"Did you call, sir?"

"Yes, Francis; tell the first lieutenant I wish to speak to him."

"In the cabin, sir?"

"Yes, here."

The boy sprang promptly to do his master's bidding, as though it were a pleasure to serve him.

The officer referred to soon entered the apartment, and respectfully saluting his superior, took the seat that was designated.

"Mr. Huford, I have been thinking that as we have got away from those rascally low latitudes, where the buccaniers seem to thrive so naturally, we had better keep if possible among people more honest than they. This has been running in my mind as we came on the coast, and I have thought that this outbreak with France would give us a chance to build up a name, and gain some renown."

"Against the French, sir?" inquired nis lieutenant.

"Yes; everything would be ready to our hands—the French are already near at hand, and I think in a week or so, with our men so well drilled and our craft under such trim, we could make ourselves felt, and capture some valuable prize, gaining gold and renown both. What do you think of the matter, sir?"

"It makes little differene to me, sir. I have got tired of the old cruising ground, to speak the truth, and should like to do something in an honourable way to gain a good name."

"How about the men—do you think they would be satisfied?"

"I'm sure of it, if a trifling addition was made in the amount of pay."

"That is easily done," said Roderick; "it is my desire that you should talk with the other officers, and report to me, as soon as may be, how the offer strikes their mind."

"I will do so, sir, at once."

The rover again dropped into a reverie as the officer departed, and thus he continued for nearly an hour, when a light knock at the cabin door aroused him. It was the lieutenant returned to make his report.

"Walk in, Mr. Huford," said the rover, recognising the knock.

"I have talked with the officers, sir, and they seem to be quite unanimous in expressing a strong desire to join the service."

"That is fortunate, then, and we will make up our minds accordingly. In the mean time, I will find an opportunity to speak to the men, and the affair will then be settled. How is the night coming on, sir?"

"Clear and bright, sir."

"Who has the next watch?"

"It is my watch, sir."

"I shall be up, directly. See the men mustered."

"Ay, ay, sir."

Soon after the rover appeared on the quarter-deck; the crew being all summoned aft, he addressed them, as follows :—

"My men,—I have not much desire to go down into the fever latitudes again, more especially when there is good game here near home. You probably all of you know that England is at war with France, and by obtaining letters of marque, I can turn our swift little craft into a government vessel at once, and thus obtain absolution for all of you as to any connection with piracy on the Spanish main. I have made up my mind to add to your monthly wages, provided you join me cheerfully in my plan against the French. What do you say to this?"

"Hurra, hurra, hurra!" exclaimed the crew, in the only language that is allowable in such a situation, either silence or cheers. They were united.

"It is well! I thought you would second me in this, as in all else; and now we may soon have a chance to test the French prowess. I have done; you may go forward."

"Hurra, hurra, hurra!" again shouted the crew, to signify their full assent.

Scarcely had the crew gone to their several stations, one watch remaining on deck and the rest below, when the look-out forward hailed the officer of the deck, saying,—

"Sail on the starboard bow, sir."

"What does she look like?"

"A ship, sir."

"What's her course?"

"Starboard tacks aboard, sir. She's on this wind, and bound up channel; we are closing with her fast, sir. You'll get her on the quarter-deck soon, sir, I think."

"Ay, ay, I have her now."

"Just off the bow, here away, sir," said the first officer to the captain.

"Let her fall off a little, so, steady," said the rover to his quarter-master.

"She looks English, Mr. Huford. Can you make out anything?"

"Not exactly, sir."

"Bring her up to hauling distance, Mr. Huford."

"Ay, ay, sir."

"And pass the word for the men to go to the guns; no drums, sir; let all preparations be in silence."

"Ay, ay, sir."

The two vessels were soon within hailing distance, when the rover, stepping upon a stanchion, asked though his trumpet,—

"What ship is that?"

"Indiaman, bound home from the east," was the reply, in bad English.

"That was the voice of a Frenchman, I will swear to it," said the rover.

"Heave to, sir, and let your captain come on board of me."

"By what authority?" inquired the officer of the Indiaman.

"By that of my own creating," was the prompt reply of Roderick, who had become convinced that he was talking to a Frenchman.

At this moment a volley of musketry was poured from the Indiaman's deck at the rover's crew, but without effect. In the next, the heavy gun amid-ships of the Spirit of the Wave, double-shotted and charged, raked the Indiaman's deck fore and aft, with terrible effect. The contest was kept up thus, the Frenchmen relying mainly upon their musketry, when the rover succeeded in laying his craft alongside the Indiaman, and as was his favourite plan, threw a section of boarders on his bows and quarter, at the same time leading the latter in person, and sweeping the deck in an instant by their impetuosity. In less than fifteen minutes after the firing of the first gun, they were masters.

On further examination, Roderick found that he had retaken a prize from the enemy of great valne, which had been captured the day before, and with a prize crew on board was now bound to some French port. Their captors were the crew of a French brigantine, or letter of marque, carrying twelve guns and a full complement, and the English ship was bound home from an East India voyage, with a rich cargo of spices, gold dust, and other valuable freight

The prize crew of the enemy consisted of some eighteen men, well armed, and it was these alone who opposed the rover, the regular ship's company being confined below. These were soon released, and put in possession of the ship, and the Frenchmen bound as prisoners in their places. The joy of the crew can better be imagined than described.

"Thank God and your valour for this," said the first mate of the Indiaman.

"Ay, we owe you everything," said the captain to Roderick.

"What name shall we report at the Admiralty, as having done us and the country this service?" continued the captain.

"Say it was Captain William Withingham, of the Spirit of the Wave."

"Withingham?" said the mate, inquiringly, while he looked eagerly at the rover.

"Ay, that is the name, my man; why do you wonder?"

"Of the Isle of Man, sir?" asked the mate.

"The same, sir," said Roderick, for he had resolved to drop his assumed name with the profession he also relinquished.

"You must be a brother, sir, of one who had deeply wronged me, but I forgive him from my heart, for his brother's sake."

"What is your name, sir?" asked Roderick.

"Levi Belt, sir."

"Levi Belt!"

"Ay, sir."

"The friend of Grace Martin?"

"That am I."

"Give me your hand," said the rover; "I congratulate you on having the regard of so kind and worthy a girl."

"Have you seen her lately, sir?"

"Within these few days, and she has told me of your troubles, which I have arranged."

"Many thanks, sir; you have been doubly my friend, and Grace and myself will both pray for blessings on your head."

The Spirit of the Wave conveyed the Indiaman into port in safety. And Captain Withingham received the highest compliment from the Admiralty office, with full legal papers for the service, and a heavy salvage money upon the cargo he had rescued.

CHAPTER IX.

"Stand to your guns, my hearts of oak,
Let not a word on board be spoke;
Victory is ours mid fire and smoke,
Be silent, and be ready.
Ram home the guns, and sponge them well;
Let us be sure the guns will tell;
The cannon's roar shall sound the knell;
Be steady, boys, be steady,"

ARRANGEMENT WITH THE ADMIRALTY.—AT SEA AGAIN.—TAKING A FORT.—HARBOUR OF L'ORIENT.—PRIZES.—NEW ENEMY.—FIGHT.—A TRUCE, A TRUCE!—SURRENDER AND VICTORY.—MEETING OF RODERICK AND ONE NO LESS CELEBRATED.

ONE week had not yet passed after Captain William Withingham, as Roderick the Rover was now called, had brought his prize safely into port, before he was again at sea cruising against the enemy. The government, anxious to avail them selves of every possible means to annoy the French, received Roderick with open arms, and by their countenance thus evinced, they endorsed his former occupations, though perhaps unwittingly. He was accorded all the rank and privilege of a captain of the regular service by the Court of Admiralty, and with his officers was duly commissioned into the service of the crown. Those who had direction of these matters were not ignorant of his prowess, or that of his well-disciplined and practised crew.

RODERICK LOOKED LIKE A STATUE AS A BOY OPENED THE CABIN DOOR.—*See page* 29.

We say that a week had not yet passed when Roderick again took the sea in his water-witch, the Spirit of the Wave. He immediately ran down channel, and close on to the French coast, so near as to entice them to throw a few shots at him from one of the forts, a random shot of which picked off one of his men. Exasperated at this, and moved by some of the old fire of a freebooter, he ran his vessel close in shore under a hot fire of shot from the enemy, landed his men promptly, stormed

and took the fort, spiked all the guns, brought away the ammunition, the com
mander of the force and most of his officers as trophies of his victory!

It was a clear bright afternoon in the year 17—. The Spirit of the Wave was
under easy sail, standing off and on, just without gun-shot of the forts at the mouth
of the harbour of L'Orient, looking out for the inward bound trading crafts that
might endeavour to make the harbour. Captain Withingham had ascertained that
there was no vessel in port fit for sea that he need fear, save one, and she was not
more than a match for him; and thus he boldly blockaded the harbour of L'Orient.
By wearing French colours, he had already succeeded in entrapping two or three
vessels, which, after stripping of all that he desired to reserve, he had sunk in full
sight of the forts, before he seemed likely to receive any attention at the hands of
the authorities at all. At length, after he had made three captures of this sort, he
observed the small craft referred to, making sail, and doubtless coming out to meet
him. He knew that she was hardly ready for sea, or she would have come out
before, but she was prepared now, and on she came.

She manœuvred for a while, trying to draw the tri-masted schooner within reach
of the guns of the fort, but without effect, for the Spirit of the Wave kept off and
on just her regular ground and beyond reach of the fort, but yet evincing no desire
to avoid an encounter with the brigantine. After tacking a while, the brigantine
lay her course for the schooner, and at the same time the distant roll of her drum,
calling her crew to quarters, came floating over the waters. This was answered on
board the Spirit of the Wave by a corresponding order, and the two vessels, well
matched in size and apparently so in armament, were fast closing with each other.
The commander of the brigantine was a man who understood his business, and as
he drew closer to his adversary, sought to gain the weather guage, and afterwards
a raking position, in both of which attempts he was foiled by the promptness with
which his plans were met, and then he commenced to fire upon the schooner from
his cannon. He was only answered by the single heavy gun that was amid-ship,
but that was worked with fearful accuracy, while the brigantine's guns, being of
lighter calibre, scarcely reached the schooner at all in the commencement of the
fight. But on came the brigantine, endeavouring to close with the Spirit of the
Wave.

"Pierre," said the captain, "you have thrown the two last of your shots
far beyond the brigantine yonder; depress your piece a little—so—that is
well ——"

"Ay, ay, sir; he has been coming up a little faster than my reckoning made out,
but I'll have him now, sir."

"Plump him right amidship, touch him in the waist, Pierre."

"Ay, ay, sir," replied the gunner, taking his range.

The next moment the splinters flew from the bulwarks of the brigantine, as she
came down hand over hand to the schooner. Captain Withingham now shortened
sail to give his enemy a chance of coming up with him at once. They were now
far enough from the fort or harbour not to fear any interruption, and as the brigantine had come boldly out to meet him with open defiance in every movement, Captain Withingham determined to give him battle, more especially as he seemed to
be so nearly equal in all respects to himself. Both vessels kept up their cannonading until close on to each other, when the brigantine tried to run the schooner
aboard, but the Spirit of the Wave promptly minding her helm, was too quick for
the manœuvre to succeed, and yet Captain Withingham was not displeased at the
evident disposition for close quarters, for he knew that his own best play was in
close quarters, hand to hand. He, therefore, chose a favourable opportunity, and
so laid the Spirit of the Wave side by side with the brigantine.

"Repel boarders on the larboard bow!" shouted Captain Withingham, and at
the same time was heard on board the brigantine,—

"Repel boarders on the starboard quarter!"

Both crews had attempted to board each other at the same time, and this was
repeated several times with vigour, until the crew of the schooner, unaccustomed
to such successful opposition, began to stare at each other in wonder. At this

moment Roderick (we must call him so now, for he was the rover again at that instant) sprang down in the waist of his vessel, and called upon his crew to follow him.

"Have we lived to be repulsed, men?" said he; "let us die on the enemy's bulwarks, or gain his quarter-deck."

"Hurra, hurra, hurra!" shouted the excited crew, promptly rallying and dashing in a body after their captain.

Captain Withingham sprang, sword in hand, upon the high bulwarks of the brigantine, followed close by his men, and literally carved his way with his sword to the deck, but every inch was fiercely contested, and though the crew of the schooner had cut their way to the quarter-deck, and twice been driven back, they had not yet placed their foot upon it. It was now the third time the crew of the schooner had driven the enemy back again to the quarter-deck, and were still gaining ground, when a voice was heard above the din of battle,—

"Now, follow me, and let every man kill his man!"

It was the captain of the brigantine; he was a brave fellow, and Captain Withingham was forced to stop for a moment to admire his spirit and bravery. Never before had he been so successfully opposed; indeed he did not hesitate to entertain for a moment the possibility of defeat, so many of his men had fallen, and so determinedly was he opposed, but as to himself, he was determined never to surrender, and if at last the event came, he would sell his life at a fearful price, for he kept the key of the magazine! He never had surrendered, and he was not about to do so now. With this determination, he seemed to be endowed with superhuman power, and led his men on, cutting down one of the enemy at every stroke. He reaches the quarter-deck, his men fall thick about him, laid low by the flashing steel of the captain of the brigantine, he was forced to retreat a fourth time, and even to the deck of his own vessel. He was soon followed by the captain and crew of the brigantine, who were emboldened by success, and another fearful contest took place, but the rovers, rallying, exerted every nerve, and drove the enemy off the deck again, following him to his own! It was a strange contest, almost without precedent, and both commanders were nearly paralysed with wonder and surprise at the singular conflict. At this juncture in the fight the two captains came close together; both seemed intent upon a personal conflict hand to hand between themselves. They were soon opposite to each other, and their reeking swords were crossed!

They paused; and for a moment seemed struck with some peculiar emotion. They made no further attempt upon each other, remaining thus for a moment, in which the two crews, seeing their commanders thus occupied, also ceased further contention as if by common consent. A strange state of affairs! Captain Withingham was the first to break this strange spell; he said,—

"Captain, I do not see but that we are pretty equally matched in every respect, and it seems to be a pity to sacrifice any more of these brave fellows—you have certainly lost forty or fifty, I have, perhaps, lost as many; shall we go on, or call it a draw game? I know not the reason, but I cannot make up my mind to strike at your life, now that we are face to face."

"It is useless to sacrifice life any further," replied the other; "and as both of us are determined upon victory if we fight on, it is useless to contend any more. If you please, we will run up the white flag."

"I am pleased with the plan," replied Captain Withingham; "or at least until we can haul off for a few repairs, and to enable us both to look after our wounded people."

"A truce! a truce!" shouted the captain of the brigantine.

"Run up the flag of truce," said Captain Withingham to his quarter-master.

And in a moment the broad white field that signifies peace was floating at the gaff of both the brigantine and schooner. This was the signal for both parties to become immediate friends, and these rough spirits, who a few moments before mingled in mortal conflict, now mingled kindly together, and shared each other's hospitality.

The two vessels soon after separated, and lay off and on near the scene of action, busily employed in making repairs and attending to the wounded. Some hours elapsed before either evinced any further tokens of hostility, when at last the Spirit of the Wave bore up and fired a gun in token of defiance, and again the combat was resumed, this time by cannonading, from which the schooner had greatly the advantage, by reason of the long gun amidship, which could be worked on any point, and which now played on the brigantine with fearful accuracy. It was not congenial with the feelings of Captain Withingham to lay off at such a distance from his enemy, but prudence forbade him to attempt another hand to hand conflict in the present disabled state of his crew. In vain did the enemy endeavour to gain close quarters on the Spirit of the Wave—she was too free for him and twice sailed entirely round the brigantine during the second conflict. The unequal contest could not last long, and the captain of the brigantine was forced to haul down his flag in token of submission, and in a few moments after the Spirit of the Wave was lying nearly side by side with her prize.

"Send your boat on board of us," hailed Captain Withingham.

"Our boats are all stove in with your shot," was the answer.

"Very well, I will come to you, then; lay your topsails a-back, you're forging a-head of me."

"Ay, ay, sir," replied the lieutenant of the brigantine.

Captain Withingham, with a strong boat's crew, soon after boarded the prize. He was received with all due courtesy and respect upon the quarter-deck of the brigantine, by the captain, who tendered to his captor the sword that he wore.

"Keep it, sir," said Captain Withingham; "never did an officer wear one more deservedly. I have roamed the seas not a little, sir, but I never saw a boat prettier managed or better fought than yours. Upon my word, I did not like to see your flag come down, I felt as though it ought to float still. You smile, but I am in earnest, sir."

"This way, sir," continued the captain, speaking to his coxwain; "run up those tri-colours again, and pull back to tell my people that it is done by my orders. Be lively, sir."

"Sir," said the captain of the brigantine, in English, "I know not how to receive this generosity, but unless I am greatly mistaken, it is the prompting of a more than noble heart."

"Say nothing of it, sir. Your vessel was too well fought to become a prize; besides, I had greatly the advantage of you."

"In that long Tom!"

"Exactly."

"I thought to myself that if you had not got that well-served piece on board your craft, one or the other of us must have gone to the bottom."

"I love to meet such an enemy as you, but it is a new thing for me to do so Pray, of what country are you—not France?"

"I am English by birth, but an American by adoption."

"Indeed!"

"Ay, I have been fitting out here at L'Orient."

"If America has many such officers as you, she is invincible!"

"Not to such as you," was the reply of the other; "what service, sir, could have so well practised yourself and men?"

After a moment's hesitation, Captain Withingham replied,—

"I have seen service in the West Indies."

"With the buccaniers?"

"Against the Spaniards," replied Captain Withingham.

"Your name, if not too inquisitive."

"I was called then Roderick the Rover."

"Ah! I have heard of that name before," said the captain of the brigantine.

"And whom, pray, have I the honour to address?" asked Captain Withingham.

"I am known in the American navy as Paul Jones."

"That is no new name to me," replied Captain **Withingham**; "let us go to your cabin and talk over these matters; strange that fortune should have thus thrown us together."

Thus saying, two of the bravest men that sailed the ocean sought the cabin together.

———

CHAPTER X.

" My honour I'll bequeath unto the knife,
That wounds my body so dishonoured.
'Tis honour to deprive dishonoured life;
The one will live the other being dead.
So of shame's ashes shall my fame be bred;
For in my death I murder shameful scorn :
My shame so dead, mine honour is new-born."

ISLE OF MAN.—MARY STACY.—LEVI BELT RETURNED TO HIS BETROTHED.—TWO DEAD BODIES IN THE GROVE.

THERE are some wild and thrillingly beautiful spots upon the Isle of Man; spots that seem in their seclusion and grandeur, to be as it were isolated from the rest of the world. The prospect from the sand-bound shores is of the most extended maritime beauty; on the north side of the island this is particularly the case. Just where a small tiny cape makes out from the shore on this side, some twenty rods above high water mark, there is a curiously formed rock, which without the aid of any artificial means has been formed by some singular freak of nature into the perfect shape of a large easy chair, with room sufficient for two persons to sit at ease within its compass. On the very night of the battle which we have described between the brigantine and the Spirit of the Wave, two persons sat in this seat of nature's forming, gazing together upon the wide outspread expanse of ocean before them, their voices only interrupted by the constant coming and receding of the surging waves, and the gentle rustling of the trees that extended nearly to the beach close in the rear of the seat. These two of whom we speak were a male and a female, holding sweet converse, and evidently lovers.

The female was young, quite young, and exceedingly fair. Her style of beauty was much after that of the lovely Grace Martin, but her eye, though beautifully expressive (a charm which is often met with in the lower classes), at times showed a fire and power of the mind that approached almost to masculine vigour. Her years might have numbered eighteen; she was tall, nearly as tall as he who was by her side, yet well formed, with the very slightest inclination to fulness of habit, just enough to make the outline of her person exceedingly graceful and handsome. Her complexion was ruddy without being coarse, but she had not the high colour that ornamented the cheeks of Grace; it was more delicate in tinge, and gave evidence of a life led more within doors. Her eyes were very black, and as we have said, at times evinced how much spirit slept within the soul they illumined, wanting only occasion to bring it forth. We might compare her disposition to the guitar; for it was as peculiar. Under the cunning hand of the musician it yields forth the most dulcet and harmonious notes; but a hardened touch begets a most discordant sound. So with the disposition; the soul that spoke through those eyes was one that would yield a corresponding note to the power that touched it. To gentleness, still greater gentleness; to kindness, a grateful affection; to love, warm, ardent devotion; but to harshness or deceit, more than a full equivalent in their own coin.   Yet you would have to look often into those dark eyes to read this, for the beauty that seemed native there and best at home, was the most confiding gentleness.   With such a being by his side, all loveliness, all passion, of the most ripened age of womanhood, gazing on the loveliness and grandeur of nature, no wonder that her companion was eloquent; he would have been a stoic who could have been otherwise.

First, his words were of the scenery around them, its beauty and noble operation; of the firmament above, now just being peopled with the myriads of stars that nightly light our world, and then as his arm stole by degrees about her waist, (so slowly that she hardly dared to resist it, lest it was unintentional), he breathed a tale of love and devotion into her more than half willing ear, and with an oily eloquence he warmly pressed his suit.   He spoke to her of the delightful union of souls, the wandering together in ideal dreams of those who truly love, the paradise that earth was to those who knew only the happiness of living for each other, until charmed like the helpless bird before the bewildering eye of the serpent, she no longer sought to disengage her waist, nor struggled in his embrace!   Her hands, before raised to prevent too close an approach of his person, now dropped and were folded across her lap, and bright pearly tears fell thickly upon them from her cheeks. And then as his thoughts became still more glowing, his words yet more persuasive, and his gentle pressure more firm, her head sunk confidingly upon his breast, and she sobbed like a child in the fulness of the passion that had grown inch by inch to possess her whole heart.

Her companion was a finely-formed, well-dressed, and intelligent young man, some few years her senior, with a high intellectual forehead, and a face that was remarkably handsome for a man.   His eyes were all that betrayed his true character; they were full and handsome in expression when set upon you, but there was a restless fire, an uneasy wandering, that told of a want of manly stability, or fixedness of purpose, a seeking for excitement to animate the spirits, a warmth of passion, which last expression was fully seconded by a full pouting lip.   A physiognomist would have read you from his countenance a full chapter of selfishness, which was to a keen observer as plain as an illumined page.   All these outward tokens of character did not belie him, for the man was Lord Charles Withingham!

"Well, Mary, you will meet me as we have agreed, to-night," he said.

"I will try to do so, but if mother should ask me where I am going, I should have to say somewhere else, and then I could not come."

"No, no, do not tell her, Mary! but come to the place as we have appointed."

"I will try."

"Till then good-by, Mary,"

"Good-by."

He drew her close to his breast, and pressed his lips to hers, a liberty he had never before taken, and thus they parted; poor Mary's cheek burning with blushes at the familiar salute.   Again, and yet again, did they meet at the stone seat, each succeeding meeting being one further step towards ruin for poor Mary, as Lord Charles coolly and cautiously prepared his victim.   Oh! the concentrated villany of a cold-blooded deed like this.

"Dear Charles," she said, (for he had taught her to address him thus familiarly), while they walked one evening in the edge of the wood that skirts the sea shore near the stone chair, "you have awakened a new world within my heart; my cares, employment, thoughts, all were so meaningless before I knew you, and are now so much of you, that I seem to have become a different being, but ah, I know myself so much your inferior in birth, education, and all that fits one to move in the circle to which you belong, that I sometimes sadly fear you cannot truly love me."

"Never doubt me, Mary, I think constantly of you by day and dream of you by night; indeed I think of little else but you, Mary, and the hour when we shall meet again."

"Do you, indeed?" she asked, looking into his eye, and leaning fondly on his arm.

"Yes, in very truth I do, Mary."

"I shall remember these words, Charles; I shall never forget them."

"Nor I, Mary."

"Ah! then how blessed I am in possessing one charm or attraction that can please or endear me to you."

Mary Stacy was completely within his power, and she fell a victim to his art!

Levi Belt soon obtained his discharge from the Indiaman after her arrival in port, and returned to the island to seek the idol of his heart, the object of his honest devotion, Grace Martin. A happy meeting was that between them. We could picture for you a scene of gentle confidence and communion between them, which would resemble much the deceitful one between Lord Charles and Mary Stacy; but while there was less apparent refinement and delicacy, there was more evident truth and honesty in every word and action. There was no mock coyness on the part of either; they had been separated for two years, and both were overjoyed at meeting again, and honestly said so to each other.

"Ah, Levi," said Grace, "I am so happy at your safe arrival, after all, your recapture from the enemy, too, by our dear kind friend."

"Now that I know of his kindness in paying my fine, and the rich gift he has given thee, it does seem to be almost a miracle."

Levi Belt seemed to have some intuitive sense of there being a good reason why Grace should dislike Lord Charles, though the secret of his attempt upon her honour had never been revealed to him, or indeed to any one save her deliverer. He seemed also to realise with greater vividness that Grace had every reason for regarding the younger brother, Lord William, as her friend, and in addition to this he had the evidence of his munificent gift to her, and the promptings of his own feelings, for his deliverance from the enemy through his bravery.

"But Grace," said Levi, "have you heard the news from the North Side?"

This was the familiar name by which this section of the island is called.

"No, Levi, what is it?"

"Not about poor Mary Stacy?"

"I have heard nothing about her; is she sick, Levi, that you ask?"

"Sick, Grace, alas! yes, she is sick, poor girl, she is crazy!"

"Crazy, what do you mean, Levi? Mary crazy! What has made her so?"

"A villain, Grace, a dastardly villain whom I have good reason to hate."

"Whom do you mean, Levi?"

"Lord Charles Withingham!"

"Hush, do not speak of him," said Grace, shuddering at the name.

"I can no longer contain the bitterness of feeling that actuates me against that man, and if he should come in my way, the consequences be upon his own head!"

"Has he wronged Mary?" asked Grace, of Levi, in a deep meaning tone.

"Yes, Grace, he has ruined her; the wreck only of poor Mary is left!"

"The heartless villain," said Grace, with honest indignation warmed to a degree of resentment against the vile perpetrator of this wickedness, that she had never felt or expressed in her own case.

"Ah! Grace, I am sometimes glad I was born a poor fisher-boy, after all, for such wickedness is the portion of the great."

"Yes, but there are many exceptions, Levi; there is Lord William."

"Lord William may be good and kind," said Levi, rather slurringly, "but he comes off the same stock after all."

"Levi!"

"Grace."

"Take back your words, or rather the insinuation against Lord William."

"Why, Grace?" asked he, in surprise, looking at her in wonder.

"Nay, I demand it of you; I have a right to do so," said Grace, with an earnestness of feeling that showed her true feelings for him she defended.

"Well, Grace, if you think him a true-hearted man, I am bound to do so."

"No brother could have been more delicate or kinder to a sister than he has been to me; he has sacrificed more than I can tell you for my sake, and next to you, Levi Belt, he is the best friend I have in the world."

"I knew you too well, Grace, not to believe you have good reason for speaking thus, and if I have spoken against Lord William, I am heartily sorry, for henceforth I shall ever respect him."

"Well said, and as manly as ever," said Grace, with a tear of pleasure in her eye.

The same evening that Grace Martin and Levi Belt held this conversation, and but a short half hour subsequent to their parting from each other for the night, the figure of a person, apparently one of the fishermen of the island, passed by the cottage at a short distance, and wended its way towards the castle. The light was rather uncertain, and the figure was therefore not recognised by Grace, who noticed it as it went by. She was standing by her door enjoying the cool, refreshing night air, and she watched the figure as it approached the castle enter a small clump of trees hard by the portal, and suddenly disappeared entirely from sight. Grace had merely given the figure a casual observation; but now she wondered where it could so suddenly and completely have hidden itself. The person of a man soon after came out from the castle and passed by it on his way to the clump of trees. When he had reached just opposite them, the figure before described again appeared, rising from the roots of one of the large trees, and approaching the person who came from the castle, seemed to Grace to take his arm; and the two then passed still deeper into the grove. It was apparent to Grace, even at that distance, that he from the castle went reluctantly with the other, who seemed, as it were, to drag him along, and in this way they disappeared from her sight. She could not distinguish either person so as to recognize them, though she tried to do so, for there was probably no one resident upon the land that she did not know; consequently she felt the more interest. But she at last retired without having seen the figures again.

On the subsequent morning two bodies were found in the wood weltering in blood, cold and stiff, with the hand of death upon them. They were soon recognised; one was poor Mary Stacy, the other, Lord Charles Withingham. A broad fisherman's dirk lay beside Mary; it had pierced Lord Charles's very heart, and he must have died in an instant. Afterwards, it was evident, she had plunged it into her own. She was disguised in part with a fisherman's coat and hat, and had sought the castle as it appeared, first to see him, tell him fully of the evil he had done, and then to take his life and her own. The spirit that had slept in her soul, and to which we referred at the commencement of this chapter, was awakened, and consumed all opposition. The cold hand of death held them both now!

CHAPTER XI.

"Our English maids are long to woo,
  And frigid even in possession!
And if their charms be fair to view,
  Their lips are slow at Love's confession.
But born beneath a brighter sun,
  For love ordained the Spanish maid is;
And who, when fondly, fairly won,
  Enchants you like the girl of Cadiz?"

CONSTERNATION ON THE ISLAND.—RODERICK AGAIN.—END OF WAR.—RECONCILIATION.—FATHER'S INTEREST WITH THE KING.—EMBASSY OFFERED.—APPOINTMENT AS MINISTER TO SPAIN.—FIGHTING FOR A LADY.

GREATER consternation and woe had never reigned in the Isle of Man. All was sorrow and grief at the castle, while the many friends of Mary Stacy (for she was the favourite of all) grieved in true earnestness for her loss. It was clear enough from the circumstantial evidence that had been gleaned of the affair that we have related in the close of the last chapter, that Mary had murdered Lord Charles, and for what reason was equally plain to all who felt any interest in the matter. Lord Withingham could make no reparation to Mary's parents for her loss; it was something beyond human power to do that, but he built the old couple, her parents, a snug cottage, and supplied them with a good store of comforts. All this was done

LORD WITHINGHAM ACCEPTS THE POST OF AMBASSADOR TO SPAIN.

in secret, and through an agent, for he would not appear to do it, lest it should be said that he endorsed the common report as to Lord Charles having betrayed and ruined Mary, before she sought this revenge upon him. But time, that healer of grief, soon sped on, with a swiftness that caused the family of Lord Withingham to forget the keenness of their sorrow, long before the parents of Mary Stacy had recovered from the first shock. The father (the mother had some time since been laid in the grave) now turned his eyes and his thoughts towards his youngest son,

Lord William, to whom he must now look for the honourable maintenance of his name and title. Never before had he considered, or treated him of any comparative importance, but now, alas! he would have given any amount to have recovered one whose absence had heretofore been unheeded. But no knowledge could be gathered of Lord Withingham, no one knew where he had gone. The old butler and Grace Martin had faithfully kept their secret.

The strange and peculiar life that Roderick the Rover had led, it would seem, should have rendered him hardened in heart and rough in exterior and speech, and altogether hardly fit for society at all. But this was not the case; his manners were still polished and easy, his words well chosen and correct, and his appearance altogether was that of one who had passed his time in courts. Thus after a few more decisive battles and gallant victories in the service we have referred to, he withdrew from it, as the war was now closed, and by particular request, made his appearance at court, where his fine manly figure, his handsome and intelligent face, and pleasing address, gave him hosts of friends at once. His great experience in the characters he had so long been associated with, for he had studied them closely, had given him an excellent understanding of human nature. The natural bravery of the disposition that actuated him, and the remarkable adventures he had participated in, all made him a great favourite at court and in society generally. The father now heard of the celebrity of his son's name and character, and hastened to court to see him. Now he could see how poorly calculated the elder brother was for the situation that he seemed designed by nature to fill, and how much superior Lord William was in all that goes to make the gentleman.

The great wealth of Lord Withingham, and his honourable and ancient name, gave him the entree at court, and also some degree of influence with his royal master, the king

Having become entirely reconciled to his son, who, indeed, told his father that he bore him no ill-will, it was agreed upon between them that the situation of ambassador to some foreign court should be sought, and if possible obtained for Lord William. This would not only be adding to his already well-spread fame, but was also well adapted to his disposition, and by the time of his return, his years and experience would be sufficiently matured for him to marry and settle for life. This was the height of his father's ambition. Therefore, backed by all the influence that he could bring to bear, he held an interview with the king; he explained and pressed his suit, and was favourably received, though he was told that at present there was no embassy unfilled, but that the first vacancy in this department should be at his service. This the king declared he should do the more readily, as he desired by some such public mark of confidence, to express his thankfulness to his son for his numerous and gallant victories in behalf of England over France in the war now just closed. Delighted with this prospect, the father thanked the king warmly, and seeking his son, related to him how the matter now stood, urging him still to remain at court, in order to take the earliest offer. The parent, having arranged these matters to their joint satisfaction, returned to his island home.

It was but a few weeks subsequent to this interview between Lord Withingham and the king, when the grand chamberlain sought Captain Withingham, and intimated to him that there was an embassy about to become vacant, which he could have by making early application to the king, after the usual form.

"Is it France?" asked Captain Withingham of the chamberlain.

"I think not," he replied; "yet I do not exactly remember."

"To Russia, perhaps?" suggested the captain, inquiringly.

"I think not; no, I am sure it was not to Russia, my lord."

"It may be Prussia, Sweden, or some other of the near kingdoms."

"It was, I believe—yes, I am sure now, it was the embassy of Spain!"

"W-h-e-w!" uttered Lord William Withingham, with peculiar meaning. He recalled his three years' depredations upon the commerce of Spain as a freebooter in the West Indies, that an enormous price had been set upon his head, and that the country had set him down as a confirmed and bloody pirate.

"Spain, Spain,—well, well, I can but try," said he to the chamberlain.

"You will get it without doubt, my lord, the king greatly favours you."

"True, true, if I like the mission to that country," said he.

"Why, my lord, it is considered the most desirable embassy within the gift of our royal master. Only the most favoured have filled it."

"Yes, for almost any one else, I should think it highly desirable; but I have a—a—constitution that will not thrive very well in Spain. Still I think the matter may be adjusted. I will see the king."

"I hope it may be agreeable to your lordship," said the chamberlain, as he politely bowed himself out of the apartment.

"Thank you, thank you," replied Lord Withingham, musingly.

Now as Lord William Withingham was not in what might be called fighting trim, he had rather have gone on any other mission than that to Spain, against whom his hand had ever been raised in the most hostile spirit, yet he reasoned to himself, "I may pass unrecognised, for my name and rank, now totally different, will blind the inquisitive; and then, too, I come the legalised representative of a nation at peace with Spain, and unless the descriptions of my person are more accurate than those which have met my eye, there can be no danger on their account either."

And thus reasoning over the matter, he argued himself to look upon it in a very different light from what he had done at first, and waiting on the king at an early moment, the affair was formally talked over and settled, the commission filled out, and himself duly installed by taking the usual oaths of office, and of allegiance to the British crown; and in less than a month after, Lord William Withingham was publicly declared to be Envoy Extraordinary and Minister Plenipotentiary from England to the court of Spain; and he immediately after departed for Cadiz.

We should fail were we to attempt to give the reader an idea of the gorgeous magnificence and splendour of Spanish high life. There is no gayer court in the world. The dames and maidens are among the loveliest that the sun shines upon, and of that voluptuousness of person and feelings (so to speak), that wholly captivates our sex. In the different grades of society there, we find, as in all countries, these divisions. The lower classes are generally virtuous, the middling classes are universally loose in their morals, and the highest of the aristocracy are far from being untainted, while a class is always found, neither at the head of rank nor yet exactly with the middling classes, where virtue seems to be the only barrier that divides them from the rest of society. His Excellency Lord William Withingham saw and realised all this; he mingled in the first circles, he was the star of attraction for all marriageable ladies at court, for it was soon whispered about that he was exceedingly wealthy, being as handsome and brave in person as he was noble in birth—qualifications to captivate the fair Castilians, above all others. His knowledge of the world, and extraordinary experience for one of his age, caused him to be courted by those much his seniors, and among others the king himself became his warm personal friend. Little did this monarch guess that Roderick the Rover was his present friend!

With so many batteries set to work upon his heart, and every one served with a pair of eyes that cut keener than grape or canister shot, how was it to be expected that His Excellency Lord William Withingham should be able to escape unscathed. The greatest trouble was that he could not choose from out such a beautiful assortment; the loveliest of any one of that host of fair creatures would have captivated the fancy of a Turk; but some how or other, Lord William would once in a while remember that he possessed such a thing as a heart; and then he would wonder to himself that it should keep so very quiet all the while, never once giving heed to all the beauty about the court.

One fair creature, whose mamma had most strongly urged her upon the notice of the English minister, and who was perfectly unconscious of the affair herself, had quite captivated his fancy; fancy we say, not love. He became quite intimate with her; they rode, walked, chatted, and danced together, until at last, to close the climax in a Spanish love affair, he was forced to fight for her. A jealous, hot-headed youth, who had known Donna Isora at school, seeing the English minister, as he thought, appropriating her entirely to himself, when it was his own hope one day to possess her, challenged Lord William to a duel. In spite of all remonstrance he found that he must fight, or be branded as a coward. The young Spaniard was of noble parents, but poor, and hence the reason that Donna Isora's mamma had not permitted their intimacy. Well, they went out to the field to fight; the swords were handed, the usual preliminaries adjusted, and the swords were crossed! The young Spaniard had counted upon his own knowledge of the weapon as being far superior to that of the English minister, but he soon found that he was completely foiled, and at last actually touched upon the breast, and his sword sent flying through the air from his hand.

"Sir, you fence remarkably well," said the conquered Spaniard, bowing low to Lord William.

"Your life is spared," replied Lord William, "perhaps there is some one else here that would like to take a little exercise. I am just warmed up, and begin to feel like it now," said he, bending his pliant weapon.

"No, no, your excellency, we would not think of permitting you to do so," said his seconds, both in a breath; for now that they knew his prowess, they did not care to test it a second time. "It would not be in accordance with your dignity," suggested the surgeon!

The probability was that Roderick the Rover was the best swordsman that ever saw the West Indies; and Lord William Withingham had in no wise forgot his practice; therefore when he saw these fellows drawing off, he determined to have some satisfaction from the affair at any rate, and so turning to them, said,—

"I must have some sport now that I am warmed up. I will take two of you at once, if that will suit you better!"

"Certainly, my lord."

"Yes, your excellency."

"If you particularly desire it."

"Just as it suits your excellency," said the seconds, the surgeon, and his late antagonist, all in a breath; each hoping that even in such a contest he would not be called upon to act. At last, however, a couple of them took their ground. Lord William, who had been accustomed to fight often half a dozen at the time, had his eyes about him; he received them, and for a while let them play at him just to show them their weakness, parrying off their thrusts as though they had been made with straws. At last having got them both in a good position for the execution of his design, he disarmed one with the quickest of thought, and struck him across his breast with the flat of his sword, while in the next instant he played the other the same trick, save that he struck him full on the breast before he disarmed him. The Spaniards are usually very adroit swordsmen, and they were utterly amazed.

"Your excellency must have seen much service, to have become so well practised," suggested the surgeon.

"Why, yes, I have used the sword some, my friend, and when any of you hear of one who would like to take a good bout in earnest, why, you know where I am to be found, that is all."

It is perhaps needless to add, that although Lord William was constantly making half the court jealous by his attention to the ladies, he never was challenged a second time while in Spain.

CHAPTER XII.

"Pray thee, maiden, hear him not,
Take thou warning by my lot;
Read my scroll, and mark thou all
I can tell thee of thy thrall.
What though a king may seek to win,
Be sure his spsrit bodes no sin.

PROPOSITION FROM A KING.—PLOT TO MEET PLOT.—APPOINTMENT IN THE ARBOUR.—SINGULAR INTERRUPTION.—ROYAL THRASHING.—WHO HAD "THE LAYING OF IT ON."—SLIGHT MISTAKE.—EXCHANGE OF LOVERS QUITE AGREEABLE.

HAVING once fully established a character for bravery, and being a perfect master of the sword, Lord William was no more troubled with challenges, although as we have said, he was constantly mingling with all the beauties of the court, heedless of their engagements with others; for, to speak the truth, after he commenced, he followed up the business for its novelty, and because he liked it. Lord William wondered at the warm interest that the king appeared to take in him; he was invited to all his majesty's private assemblies, dinner parties, and frequently to dine alone with the king, who seemed actuated by some secret purpose in a desire to gain the full confidence of the English minister.

"My lord," said the king to him on one occasion, when they were alone, "I have something on my mind that I wish to reveal to you."

"I pray you speak freely, sire."

"First, then, my lord, do you affect this Donna Isora?"

"No further, sire, than as a friend, a kind and gentle friend."

"You bear her no passion, no warmer regard than this?"

"None, sire."

"Then listen to me; I must possess her! I have long marked and loved her; the queen does not suspect me—and if by your aid I could gain the Donna Isora's favour, ask what you will it shall be granted to you!"

Lord William was taken completely aback by such a proposition, and did not know how to act. His first impulse was to punish the man who could make so vile a proposal to him, upon the spot, but prudence forbade this, and in an instant of time his plan of conduct was formed, and turning to the king, he replied,—

"Any matter that I can serve you in, I beg you will command me."

A moment's consideration caused Lord William better to understand the matter, for he knew very well that the king was a young hot-headed Castilian, accustomed to all manner of intrigues of this sort, and that it looked far less heinous to him, born and bred in that passionate clime, than it did to one like himself who had been eaaly taught to cherish and protect virtue. "And yet," thought he, "I should like to punish his majesty in some way for his rascally design." Acting upon this purpose, and while his plan of action was yet unformed, he replied as we have seen.

"Well, then," continued the king, in reply to his remark, "it is very evident that Donna Isora is fond of your company, and you must make an appointment to meet her in some quiet place which I will designate, and in room of yourself, why, just send me as your proxy. The time and place befitting, leave the rest to me."

"I think I understand you, sire. You will communicate to me the time and place, and then I shall know how to act."

"Yes, yes, my lord, I will send you word when I have arranged it."

"If you please," replied Lord William, bowing himself out of the apartment.

"The rascal," muttered he to himself, as he left the audience chamber, "a king, a man who has seen nearly forty years experience, a noble cavalier, to engage in uch business as this, and use me, too, as a cat's-paw! Egad, I can hardly contain my resentment; but stay, I will fix him yet, or else I am vastly mistaken."

That night, Lord William and Isora met at a grand ball given by one of the nobility, at which the king also appeared. As usual, the English minister danced several times with Donna Isora, and promenaded the spacious halls with her upon his arm, after mingling in the giddy mazes of the waltz. The king watched them, and more than once sought to exchange glances of intelligence with Lord William, but to no effect, for the English minister seemed determined not to understand him. And yet he did do so, but pretended this ignorance solely to tease and annoy the king, which he accomplished most admirably. At last the ball broke up, and all retired to their homes. Donna Isora entered her mother's vehicle, and drove away with her for home, while Lord William, after handing her into it, turned to walk to his own lodgings; but scarcely had he passed a single square before he was overtaken by a person who laid his hand on the English minister's arm; he turned—it was the king.

"How delightfully she looked and danced to-night," said he.

"Whom, sire!" asked Lord William, with provoking indifference.

"Whom? why, the Donna Isora, to be sure," replied the king.

"Ah yes, sire, I quite forgot, she was very beautiful."

"I am all impatience, my lord, to bring about our arrangement."

"Have you selected the time and place?" asked the minister.

"Yes, both, and will designate them to you now."

Saying which, he explained to Lord William the hour for keeping up the appointment, and the place where it should be holden. A quiet wing of the palace devoted to botanical purposes was the place named, and the minister agreed to make an appointment with the Donna Isora in accordance, when the king in place of himself was to come disguised in the minister's cloak and hat, so as to prevent discovery from any one else, and to enable him to carry out his plan the more perfectly. All this arranged, Lord William met Donna Isora as usual, and the appointment was made on some slight pretext, quite sufficient to render Isora punctual, however; for to tell the truth, she was well pleased with the attention that she received from the distinguished Englishman. This done, Lord William sat down and addressed a note to the cavalier with whom he had fought the duel, saying that his excellency the English minister had made an assignation with the Donna Isora at such a place, specifying the spot referred to, and that it would well become a true Spaniard to be on the spot to chastise the villanous fellow. The note was signed "A friend," and sent so as to be duly and safely received. Signor Nortez, who had been so completely foiled at the sword by Lord William, bethought himself on the receipt of this note, that now there was a glorious chance for revenge; for he reasoned that by being punctually there, he would not only be able to break up the meeting between him and Donna Isora, but he might also chastise the minister with his cane before he could prepare to defend himself; and this he determined upon.

It was nearly midnight when the Donna, leaving the gay halls of the king's bower strolled into the garden wing of the palace grounds to meet by appointment the English minister. He was also present during the evening, and had a few moments before left the halls, which Donna Isora took as a signal for her also to depart and meet him. The lady sauntered slowly on until she came to the spot sheltered by thick trellises of vines, woven so as to form an arbour. Stepping in, she seated herself, and with her pretty feet played with the beams of the bright, clear moonlight that struggled through the vines, and shot across the floor. Her eyes were downcast, and she did not observe the person approach her who now stood there until he was pausing before her; half raising her head, and recognising the well known hat and cloak of him she expected, she said,—

"How beautiful is the night, and how sweet the hour for meeting those with whom we can enjoy such things."

"It is beautiful, and it seems to greet its queen smilingly, as she ventures forth at this hour to enjoy it."

Donna Isora started and looked up for an instant, but dropped her eyes again to the earth as she seemed satisfied upon some doubtful point that had entered her mind, saying,—

"Were you weary, or ill to-night, my lord, that you looked so reserved?"

"I was absorbed in thoughts of thee, fair Donna Isora," replied her companion, taking a seat by her side, and gently placing his hand about her waist as he did so.

Now Isora would not have repulsed such a movement from Lord William; but the very movement led her to doubt that it could be him, and looking earnestly in the face of him by her side, she saw that it was the king. She knew not what to do; she dared not to offend him, she could wish herself anywhere else at that moment, more particularly as she momentarily expected Lord William himself. She hesitated, struggled, and endeavoured to disengage herself from the king. Just at this moment another person appeared at the door of the arbour. He suddenly entered, seized the man by the collar who had been sitting so near to Isora, and pulling him by main force from his seat, laid a small cane so smartly about his head and ears that he was forced to cry for mercy at the very top of his voice!

At length, pausing to take breath, the Spaniard looked at him whom he had taken to be the English minister full in the face, when he exclaimed in a tone of the greatest horror and alarm,—

"Holy mother, it is the king! it is the king! what have I done?"

"Peace, prattling fool," said the king, "have you not done evil enough already, but you must alarm the whole palace?"

"Pardon, pardon, a thousand times pardon," said the kneeling Spaniard.

"Rise," said the king, panting for breath, from the bruises he had received, "and but hold your foolish tongue about the matter, and you may go in quiet."

Signor Nortez made the best of his way from the palace, cursing all the saints in the calendar at his misfortune.

In the meantime and during the confusion that was going on, Donna Isora made her escape, but had proceeded only a few rods when she was met by Lord William who was apparently just coming to keep his appointment, and who coolly said,—

"Ah, Donna Isora, did you get tired of waiting for me?"

"Nay, in good sooth, not I, but a quarrel taking place there, I have left."

"A quarrel, Isora, about what; not about thee, is it?"

"It would be hard for me to say what it is about, my lord, but in faith I must tell you that I mistook the king for you, until he became familiar, and then some one from without interfered and gave him a most thorough and strenuous beating!"

"Indeed!" said the innocent (?) Lord William, "this is bad business."

"It is bad, indeed, when the king is beaten in his own palace."

The English minister waited upon Donna Isora to her home, and the king was not to be seen for some days after this eventful evening! As to Signor Nortez, some how or other he rose greatly in favour with the king, who gave him a lucrative office, and conferred upon him many honours. The fact was, Signor Nortez held the king's secret!

At last, Lord William tired of Isora, for he had used her as a child would a favourite plaything, until sick and tired of it, he casts it away. He grew less and less attentive, until the cunning mother seeing how matters worked, now permitted the attention of Signor Nortez, whose office and income now gave him no little consequence in connection with the particular friendship of the king!

Donna Isora, brought up like most other Spanish maids of high rank, was equally well pleased with Signor Nortez, and the two soon became the best of friends. It was for the king's interest to have their good will, otherwise they could report the circumstances of the arbour scene to his great mortification, and therefore he not only kept Signor Nortez in office, but even hastened on the marriage of Donna Isora with him, making her a magnificent wedding present, on the occasion of their nuptials.

"How did the meeting pass off in the arbour?" asked Lord William of the king, one day when they were alone.

"The meeting, let me see," said the king, pretending to forget what the minister referred to.

"The meeting with Donna Isora, that we arranged together, sire."

"Ah, yes, yes, well, there was a trifling mistake in that affair, owing to an interruption, but your part was well performed."

"A mistake, sire, I am very sorry. I thought I had arranged the matter perfectly on my part!"

"You did, my lord, I have no fault to find at all."

Lord William bowed low, and passed from the palace, but as he did so he could not suppress a malicious chuckle, for this was the king whom he had fought so strenuously and successfully on the ocean, and to be able thus to outwit him on land was a pleasure that he had never anticipated. Thus ended the adventure between Donna Isora, Lord William, and the king. Isora found a husband, the king a sound drubbing, and Lord William sport to his heart's content.

Though we may be inclined at times to play with the heart of another, still, sooner or later, we are sure to find that we have one ourselves; and thus it was with the English minister, as we shall show you, gentle reader, in the next chapter.

———

CHAPTER XIII.

> " Mysterious Love !
> Thy presence is around me, and I feel
> All it's o'ermastering influence. A chain—
> A viewless chain—binds my stern spirit down
> To more than woman's gentleness. A spell
> As 'twere of voiceless music, through my soul
> Steals with a soft delight unfelt before."

TIRED OF THE EXCITEMENT OF COURT.—THE HOLIDAYS.—LORD WILLIAM'S FAITHFUL VALET.—THE INVITATION AND ACCEPTANCE.—LOVE AT FIRST SIGHT.—LADY CALDERON.—THE ENGLISH MINISTER LOSES HIS HEART.—A LORD IS TO BECOME A PAGE!

EVERY pleasure will clog sooner or later when too freely indulged in, and thus it was with Lord William Withingham, the English minister. He had fully participated in all the dissipation of the court, until he had grown heartily tired and wearied of its attractions. Thus actuated, he pined in secret for a renewal of the wild life he had led in former days upon the sea, and to speak honestly, a thought even crossed his mind as to the possibility of its renewal! But this was of course out of the question, for he could no longer fight a nation whose hospitality he had shared, and there were no other wars in Christendom that he could mingle in with honour and credit. Thus pent up within the bounds of every day life, he seemed to chafe like a caged tiger who pines for the tangled jungle and his freedom. He mingled less with the court, studied for his amusement, so that he became more thoroughly perfect in the language, and reviewed in course all his former studies, until he seemed to have completely exhausted every resource of amusement within his reach. At this juncture a new aspect was given to his fortunes by a change in all his feelings.

It was now the gayest season of the year; the holidays had commenced, and the nobility seemed to vie with each other in the splendour of the nightly entertainments that were constantly occurring. Lord William Withingham's table was covered with unnoticed invitations, for he, as we have said, was quite weary of himself and everybody else. When he left London for the Spanish court, he had taken into his employ as his valet, the lad Francis, whom the reader has once before met on board the Spirit of the Wave. This boy was Spanish by birth, and thoroughly understood the language, being remarkably bright and intelligent. He was attached to the ship's company whom Lord William disbanded at the

DONNA ISORA AWAITS LORD WITHINGHAM IN THE BOWER.

close of the war, but, having become warmly attached to his captain, he begged that he might be retained in his employ as a servant. His father had taken him out to the West Indies, where his own life was sacrificed to the rigorous colonial laws, and the boy, indignant at the punishment of his father, ran away and joined the Freebooters against his own country. Hearing of Roderick the Rover, he sought him out, and was received first as a cabin boy and afterwards as a clerk.

Until he became himself perfectly *au fait* in the language, the boy Francis was of inestimable service to him; we say boy, but he was now fully nineteen, a fine manly fellow, and thoroughly devoted to Lord William's interest. He had come in one morning, as was usual, to his master's apartment. Lord William had just risen, and sat with a loose wrapper about him, tossing over his various unanswered invitations. At last one struck his attention; it was a blazoned note bearing the family arms of the sender upon it, and he opened and read it, then laid it aside with the rest. It was from some new family that he had not yet visited.

"Beg pardon, sir," said Francis, eyeing the coat of arms on the envelope of the invitation just laid aside, "but is not that from the family of Calderon?"

"Yes, Francis, I believe it is," said his master, languidly.

"Won't you answer it, sir? They are of the best blood in Spain, and have only come to town for the holidays."

"No, Francis, I am tired of this life of inactivity."

The valet's eye sparkled with animation, as he seemed to read the meaning of his master's words in his expression of countenance.

"Do you ever think, sir, of those cruisings in the low latitudes?"

"Ah, Francis," replied his master, "yes, often, often," and the English minister sighed to himself as he remembered his life of a Rover.

"Why not return to it, sir?" asked Francis, timidly.

"Why, my boy, because circumstances have conspired to mew me up among the circles of false delicacy and mock refinement. Francis, I would give more than I can now command to be once more on the quarter deck of the Spirit of the Wave, with all my old crew about me, an enemy in sight, and everything set that would draw, in chase of her." As Lord William spoke he rose with the excitement, and walked the room as though he had indeed been on his own quarter-deck.

"If I might venture to suggest, sir, I hope you will attend the levee of the Calderons; it is the talk of all the town, and would serve to amuse you at least. They say the lady is very beautiful."

"That least of all I care for now, Francis; I am surfeited."

"I want to say that you will be there, sir, I am asked so often."

"Well, well, I will go, Francis, if only to please you."

"Thank you, sir, and if you do but recover your spirits again by it, I shall be the happiest fellow in all Castile."

Francis, who really loved his master, was overjoyed at this promise that he would attend the levee in question, for he found that since his master had abstained from society, he had grown melancholy and absent. He applied himself therefore with unwearied diligence to prepare his proper suit, and when night came to get him off in the very best style.

The English minister had hardly entered the splendid apartments, which would vie with the palace itself in the richness of their furniture and fixtures, when his eyes became fixed upon a daughter of the Calderon family, whose beauty was different from anything that he had met in Spain. He was riveted in his attention; he did not speak to her, did not seek an introduction, but gazed as though entranced upon her, and now and then he would close his eyes, as if to remember himself and then gaze upon her again. He was one of the last to leave the halls of gaiety as day was breaking the following morning, and when he did so, it was in a stupor, he seemed like one under the effects of a powerful narcotic. Francis was alarmed about him for a while, and urged him to retire to rest, but he refused, partook sparingly of a slight meal, and calling for a horse, rode away for miles from the city, lost in meditation. The fair creature he had seen had charmed him. It was love, deep, burning, consuming love, at first sight!

"Can God have made so beautiful, so angelic a creature, in a world so heavenly, and not have given her a mind to correspond with her outward lovliness," he asked himself. "I might easily have won her ear last night for a while at least, but I dared not break the spell, I feared the charm would be dispelled. If she be like the greater portion of these Spanish belles, I could easily win her heart, from my station and known wealth; but ah, it is not a heart thus acquired that I can love, I would be loved for myself alone. What emotions did she awaken in my heart! Never before have I been so moved save once, when my heated imagination conjured up an angelic phantom in a walking dreaming hour on the shores of Cuba. God of heaven, how like were my sensations last night, to those I experienced on that occasion."

It was plain enough that Lord William had completely lost his heart, and thus he communed with himself, until at last he returned at the close of the day to his apartments. Francis was there to meet him, he saw that some new emotion had possessed his master, who was more absent and thoughtful than before.

"Francis," said he abruptly, addressing his valet—"Do you know aught of this family of Calderon whom I visited last night?"

"Only that they are the noblest in all Castile, save the royal family."

"How did you first hear of the levee they gave last night."

"Of Antoine, the valet, sir,"

"Do you know him?" asked Lord William, musing.

"Yes, sir, I was his friend in boyhood."

"Have you influence over him?"

"I think so, my lord; as I said, we were mates at school together, and I always espoused Antoine's quarrels as my own."

"Francis, come hither."

"Yes, my lord."

"Do you think you could arrange a little matter for me that requires secrecy, judgment, and cool calculation."

"If a hearty desire to do all that may please you, my lord, be any guarantee, then I can pledge myself to the purpose."

"I believe you, my good Francis, we have been too long together not to be more to each other than mere servant and master."

"Thank you, my lord," said the respectful valet.

"Well, Francis, this family of Calderon live in the suburbs of the city, or rather a few leagues from it. They have a large retinue, with many servants; all this you know. The lady Calderon is mistress now of the household, for her father has been ordered by the king to a distant province on matters of state. So much I have learned from a reliable source. This Antoine you speak of, what do you say is his situation?"

"He is page and valet to the Lady Calderon, my lord."

"Very good; now, Francis, I want that situation myself!"

"My lord!" said the astonished valet, with uplifted hands.

"I say that I want that situation myself, and I shall rely upon you to prevail upon Antoine to resign his place, and more than that, to recommend me for his substitute!"

"I do fear, sir, that it cannot be done, for he loves his mistress, with the most devoted respect, and has been raised from boyhood in the family."

"No matter, Francis, it must be done, and you know me well enough to understand that when I have fixed upon it, it will be accomplished sooner or later b some means or other. There is a purse containing fifty doubloons; take it an employ the contents for this purpose. Antoine must think me a poor, but we educated English friend of yours, a man who can well fill his place. Buy him ol if only for a while, but do not trust him with one word of the secret—that would not do at all."

"But, my lord, you will be missed here, your office will be vacated."

"I can easily arrange that, Francis, by giving out that I am away on a shor visit to a neighbouring country."

"True, sir, if we can only get Antoine to consent to the business."

"That I shall leave to you, Francis, and for your reward, you shall act in m absence as my representative, and receive the full pay for the time."

"You are ever so generous, sir," said the grateful valet.

"Say no more of it, but hasten to see Antoine, and then report to me what he result of your conference."

"I will do so at once," replied Francis, departing on his errand.

We should say here, in explanation, that Lord William had retained Francis more as private secretary than as a valet, after all, for he had several other servants in his household, but yet this is the title that we have thought the most appropriate for him.

After he had left the room, the English minister paced his apartment, talking half-aloud to himself.

"Yes, if she can love me truly for myself, she can as well do so in one station as another. It is the only way that I can truly and honestly test her affection. It may be that I shall be rejected, if so, I had rather it would be in any other guise than that of my office. How delicious to think that I shall be constantly near her, ready at her slightest call to hand a book, to read to her, do anything that her gentle and sweet fancy may prompt. Ah! if my good angel does but approve in this, I am blessed for life!"

The minutes all seemed hours until Francis again returned. He had faithfully done his errand, had seen Antoine, and after a great deal of persuasion and urging, he had at last consented to the proposal offered by Francis, but stated that it would be impossible for him to do so until their return from a short journey inland that was to be commenced that very afternoon. He expected the family would be absent for six weeks, or nearly that, and on their return he promised, if his heart did not fail him, he would leave the Lady Calderon's service, and recommend Francis's "friend" to the situation he left.

But it was a great struggle in the heart of the honest fellow between his love for his mistress, the persuasion of Francis, his attachment to the service, and the glittering doubloons that his friend jingled in his ears.

But, as we have said, he at last consented, and so Francis reported his errand to his master when he returned.

"Six weeks," said Lord William; "they will be years to me."

"I was thinking, sir, as I came along, that after all, it will, perhaps, be as well that this delay shall take place, for it will be necessary for you to adopt some disguise that will not lead you to be detected by any courtier who may chance to see you."

"True, true, I have hardly thought of detection, Francis."

"You have worn no beard since you have been in Spain, sir. Why not cultivate your moustaches during these six weeks, retire into the country, assume an appropriate dress, and thus render more complete your disguise. You look very differently with moustaches, sir."

"It is a good idea, Francis, and I shall adopt it," replied his master.

"I believe that I have completely arranged the matter, so far as it relates to Lady Calderon's private valet, but that is a small part of the business, my lord, as there will be many curious eyes bent upon you, and unless the disguise is perfect, detection may follow."

"You are thoughtful, Francis, and I need, for the first time, I believe, some one to do the cool head work for me. It is a new feeling that prompts me; I have no one else to confide it to, and Francis, I shall depend much upon your discretion."

"Thank you, my Lord, for this confidence," he replied.

"I have plans yet uncompleted, Francis, for your preferment and promotion. I have known you for a long period; you have always been efficient and faithful, and I shall soon have occasion to test both of these qualities still further, but I shall do it with confidence."

"If devotion to your interest, my lord, is any guarantee, I am well recommended in that, at least."

"Come to me an hour hence, when I have thought over my plans, and we will arrange a final course of action."

"I will, my lord," replied the devoted Francis.

Lord William then sat himself down and thought over the plan he would pursue. It was a bold deed that he contemplated, and one that might fail, and all be discovered; but he was determined thus to test the truth of a heart, whose owner had already completely captivated his affection. We shall see how his stratagem succeeded.

CHAPTER XIV.

"I said it was a wilful, wayward thing,
　And so it is, fantastic and perverse!
Which makes its sport of persons and of seasons,
Takes its own way, no matter right or wrong,
It is the bee that finds the honey out,
Where least you dream 'twould seek the nectarcous
　　store,
And 'tis an arrant messenger, this same love—
That most outlandish, freakish faces wears,
　To hide his own!"

PLANNING AND EXECUTING THE PLOT.—A COUNTRY RESIDENCE.—RIPENING OF THE PLAN.—THE LADY AND THE NEW PAGE.—HAWKING, READING, AND COMMUNING.—ADVENTURE WITH THE SPANISH BANDITTI.—THE FIERCE ENCOUNTER. —THE ESCAPE.—THE PURSUIT.—RODERICK'S FATAL SHOT.

GREAT care was necessary in the planning of his object, and now that he saw six weeks before him, in which he could do nothing else to divert his mind, Lord William resolved to make his arrangements in the most careful manner. A place for board was obtained at some four leagues from the city, the suit of a common page was procured, with a few books to while away the hours, and thus equipped, the English minister buried himself for a few weeks in solitude. It was the first time for many years that he had enjoyed the opportunity of self-examination, and the quiet that can only be found in the seclusion of the country. He read, walked, and communed alone, until he felt refreshed from the rest, the natural rest he obtained. His sleep was sweet, his appetite good, his mind clear and invigorated, and even his handsome face seemed to have received additional interest aad expression, from this new mode of life. Six weeks were thus soon passed away—a dark silky moustache curled above Lord William's upper lip, his long hair was trimmed more modestly, and his high forehead left exposed. His dress, too, of the simplest kind—all served to render imperceptible his disguise.

Francis came according to appointment, as he said, "to show his English friend where he could get employment in the occupation which he had been brought up to perform;" and paying his bill at the honest cottager's where he had boarded, with a liberality that made the honest host offer to return a portion of the sum, they departed for the castle of the house of Calderon. Antoine was ready to receive them, but with a woeful countenance, for he had already half repented his bargain. The premium was paid into his hand, and he ushered the new page into the presence of the Lady Calderon.

She was reclining upon a velvet couch, in a spacious and richly furnished room, a book was half closed in one hand, and she seemed to be musing on some matter which she had been reading. She hardly turned at the entrance of Antoine, but seemed to know his errand, and said gently,—

"Is this the new page, Antoine, whom you recommend?"

"It is, my lady; and his experience, I hope, may render him more serviceable to you than I have been; but he cannot love your service better than I do."

"You have always been faithful, Antoine, and must send me word when my name will be of service to you."

The page approached, and kneeling before her, bade her good-bye, with honest tears in his eyes, declaring that he should ever pray for her. A heavy purse from the lady closed the scene, and went far to reconcile the ex-page to the loss of his situation, though he went away very sad.

The Lady Calderon then turned to look upon the new comer. He stood leaning gracefully by the door, with eyes bent upon the floor, and a heart that beat so quickly as almost to make him tremble. She had turned languidly towards him, with the purpose of a few interrogations, but when her eyes rested upon him, she half rose from the couch, and leaning upon her arm, gazed fixedly upon him for a moment, with a show of interest that it was, perhaps, well he did not see; but she recovered her calm self-possession again instantly, saying,—

"Your name?"

"Roderick, my lady," replied the page, respectfully, raising his large, expressive full eyes upon her.

This time she rose entirely to an upright position, and gazed fixedly upon him, as if some peculiar chord had been touched in her heart by the sound of his voice, but the pause was momentary only, and the beautiful lady was again herself, calm and serene in her loveliness.

"Roderick, it is an easy name; I like it well. Has Antoine instructed you as to your new duty?"

"In part, my lady," replied the page; "and with a share of kindness on your part for one who has been long out of service, I hope to succeed."

"You are well recommended by Antoine," she replied; and touching a bell-cord by her side, a servant appeared, whom she directed to show the new page to a certain apartment, and fit him with a suit of page's livery, after the colours of her house. Roderick (for so he is again called) followed the servant to be clothed in the Calderon livery!

He was soon completely fitted in a dress that became his light and graceful form to perfection. He seemed in form and manner as though he had been designed by nature for such gentle service as he now assumed, and when he appeared again before his lady in full dress, she could not avoid an expression of pleasure As he entered the room, he saw that the book which she held had fallen upon the floor, and advancing gracefully, he picked it up, offering it to her. She extended her hand to take it, but afterwards motioned it away, saying,—

"You may lay it by, Roderick, my eyes weary of the type."

"May I not read to you, my lady?" he asked, respectfully.

"Yes," said she, pleased at this thoughtfulness, and designating the page where she had broken off.

Roderick opened the volume, and sitting upon a cushion near her feet, read in a low, musical voice, page after page. He understood the Spanish thoroughly, and pronounced it like a native, while the slight foreign brogue that marked his articulation but rendered it the more interesting The book was one of those highly wrought, and chivalrous romances of the sixteenth century, and with such an apt conception as Roderick possessed, it was rendered so life-like, as to seem to the Lady Calderon almost real. At last, though in the midst of a chapter, and at a point where the interest was at its height, she requested him to pause, adding,—

"You must be tired now, Roderick; you may lay by the book."

It was not for one in his situation to reply to this, but he felt the meaning of it. Did she already, then, feel sufficient interest in him not to over-task his powers even in so slight a matter as this? He nursed the idea fondly!

Thus for many days he read to her, attended her in her horseback rides, her hawking excursions, and in short, performed fully the part of a confidential and trusty page. He should be old enough for a protector in part, and yet not too old to be of service in all that appertains to such employment. Never was lady better served; her very wishes seemed anticipated, the rarest flowers, and those which were her favourites, were always fresh upon her toilet, her favourite hawks were never before so well trained, her horses seemed in exactly the right order for her rides, the bridle was easier to her hand, the saddle firmer and softer than before,—in short, everything bore tokens of a constant care for her pleasure.

It was impossible for her not to observe this, nay, to feel that it was no common thoughtfulness that accomplished all this. Waking or dreaming, the noble page was her constant thought. More than once had she detected his handsome eye bent upon her with a devotion of feeling in its expression that it was impossible to misinterpret, and yet there was not one step beyond the strictest bounds of respect ever made by the page. He was the same devoted, thoughtful, and attentive servant. He was her almost constant companion, and seemed now to have grown to be actually necessary to her happiness!

Before others and the world, there was, if possible, even a greater distance observed between the page and his mistress than was usual in their respective situations, but when alone, though there was a strange feeling of restraint that seemed to be growing upon the manners of the Lady Calderon, still all austerity was gone, and an unmistakeable air of kindness had taken full and complete possession of her bearing. Not a glance or expressive movement escaped Roderick; though he seemed to be utterly unconscious of them all, they were each treasured as priceless in his heart.

The excitement of hawking and following the birds in their flight had led the party of Lady Calderon one day far away from the castle, and into a district not celebrated for its good character. Three leagues, at least, lay between the castle and the party, when at last the sport was relinquished, and the hawkers turned towards home. The party consisted of the lady, and three servants with the hawks, game, &c., and Roderick.

They had ridden but a short mile on their homeward way, when just as they ascended a little rising knoll, they discovered in the valley below them three horsemen, riding to meet them. It needed no second look to tell the little party that they were Spanish brigands! It was a lonely neighbourhood, just the spot for a bloody deed, and for an instant the colour deserted the cheek of the lady. Roderick saw it in an instant, and in the next was by her side.

"My lady, you are a bold horsewoman—I may say it now, perhaps,—and you ride better than any other female I ever saw. We all know who those are coming this way. These three servants are worse than nothing, therefore we can make no combined resistance. I have this rapier, it is light, but I have handled one before. Let us ride together until we are close upon them, I will then dash forward and attract their attention by engaging one or more of them with the sword, and in the meantime you can dash by them, and your roan will distance any horse in the district. I think we may thus confront them."

"You speak promptly, and to the purpose, Roderick, like one accustomed to emergencies, but I cannot leave you to their revenge!"

"Fear not for me, dear lady, I am equal to three such as these."

"I cannot leave you behind in this manner, Roderick," said Lady Calderon, blushing in spite of herself at the interest she betrayed.

"I pray you, lady, give heed to my advice, they are at hand!"

"May our holy mother protect you, Roderick!" she said, seating herself firmly in the saddle, and reining in her horse to put him to his mettle.

On came the brigands, with drawn swords, while Roderick, turning to the servants, said,—

"Wait until our lady has fairly the start, then dash after her, and if pursued, turn all three of you and oppose the foremost horseman; by this means our lady will be enabled to escape. Be faithful, for by the saints above us, I will take the life of him who flies in any other direction, with my own right hand. Now mark, and be ready!"

Hardly had he finished speaking, when the two parties met.

"Halt!" thundered forth the leader of the brigands, while at the same time the three arranged themselves across the way in such a manner as to stop the passage.

Whispering a word in the ear of the lady, Roderick bade her dash by the nearest horseman on the left, while he should engage him. The nearest robber extended his hand to seize her bridle, when a quick blow from Roderick's rapier severed it from the wrist, and the lady passed by unharmed. Roderick's animal was restless in the extreme, and one good resulted from this, as neither of the unwounded men could get a chance to wound him. The wounded horseman was turning to follow the Lady Calderon, and Roderick gave the servants, who had thus far remained inactive, orders to dash off and intercept him, and the robber was easily overcome by them.

Roderick had already so wounded one of the horsemen, that he had dismounted, and drawing a pistol, the shot struck Roderick's horse, and he fell dead. Thus dismounted, the leader of the banditti thought him safe enough, more particularly as he saw also at this moment his own man rising to his feet, and dashed off in pursuit of the lady.

Roderick was in such fear lest the robber should overtake the Lady Calderon, that he heeded not the approach of the wounded bandit by his side, until he had struck a strong blow with his sword, which entered his side just on the ribs, making a severe flesh-wound. This brought him to himself again, and in a moment after, the robber lay dead at his feet! Hard by he saw the robber's horse grazing— was on his back in an instant, and after plying the rod and steel for some minutes, found himself coming up with the leader of the banditti. Roderick was already faint from loss of blood, but he still urged on his panting steed till he was nearly up with them. The servants had dispersed in different directions, believing this their safest mode. The robber chief was now close by the side of the Lady Calderon. The lady had not until now turned her head for some time, but now she did so, and could almost reach the head of the robber's horse with her whip. A little in the rear, came Roderick, almost exhausted, his horse on the full run, and his hand steadily grasping the rein. It was a strange sight to see them thus flying, as it were, through the air. Roderick alters his position a little by the turn of the rein, getting more to the side of the robber, and out of line with his mistress; he draws a pistol from the holster before him, aims at the robber and fires, while a film is yet gathering over his eyes, and the next instant both the robber and the page fell to the ground!

CHAPTER XV.

"A league is still a compact, and more binding
In honest hearts where words must stand for law,
And in my mind, there is no traitor like
Him whose domestic treason plants the po'nard
Within the breast which trusts to his truth."
        Preach, will you Mac?
        Do it, and I'll kill the boy!"

SECRETARY OF THE ENGLISH MINISTER.—AN UNLOOKED FOR DANGER.—"I KNOW YOU, SIR!"—AN OLD ACQUAINTANCE, AND A TRAITOR!—THE SECRETARY IN TROUBLE.—SEEKS LORD WILLIAM.—THE PLAN OF ACTION.—THE APPOINTMENT AND THE KEEPING OF IT.

FRANCIS, the confidential secretary of the English minister, had not been idle during his master's absence, but endowed with the title of *vice*, or secretary of legation, he improved the opportunity to put his master's affairs in the best condition, and also to exercise the duties of his office with dignity and a scrupulous regard to justice. These qualities soon drew him into notice, and he mingled in the first circles, receiving but little less compliment and respect than his more accomplished master had done. To the constant inquiry for him he had but one answer—that he had gone to visit a distant section, from whence he would return after the lapse of three or four months.

RODERICK, AS THE PAGE, READING TO LADY CALDERON.

Francis had, until his promotion, kept much by himself, as there were some persons in the city who had been in the colony at the time of his father's death, and he wished to avoid their recognition; for although he had changed with some years of time, still his features were sufficiently peculiar to lead him to fear so unpleasant a meeting. He had, therefore, as we have said, kept somewhat secluded, but now, presuming upon the dignity of his office, he felt less fear of being known.

It might have been some six weeks after Lord William had donned his page's suit, that a singular circumstance occurred which startled Francis not a little; and even Lord William would have been aroused had he been the one to meet it, in room of his trusty and faithful secretary.

Francis was sitting in the office one day, when a couple of sea-faring men applied for admission—one a Spaniard, and the other an Englishman. The two had been quarrelling about some small debt, and at last had agreed to leave the matter to the settlement of the English minister, as it related to service in an English vessel. Francis thought that he would hear the matter, and if it was in his power to arrange it, they both should receive justice in the case. They were, therefore, permitted to come in before him.

They stated their case, and while they did so, Francis observed that the Englishman eyed him with the most intense scrutiny, noting every word that he spoke, and every movement that he made. At last, the decision was made, and all parties seemed satisfied, when the Englishman, drawing a little nearer to the secretary, said,—

"Can I have a word in private with you, sir?"

"Yes. You may retire," he said, signifying his wish to the person who had entered with him who now asked his private ear.

The apartment being cleared, the Englishman approached, and said,—

"I know you, sir!"

"What of that?" asked Francis, endeavouring to hide the slight confusion that overcame him for a moment at the deep meaning tone of the Englishman.

"Why, only that if the king of Spain knew that also, you would be quartered, and your limbs hung at the gates of the city."

"You talk like a crazy man," replied Francis.

"Perhaps you do not remember Lawrence Bray, on board the Spirit of the Wave, in the West Indies?"

"Yes, I think I do," replied Francis, coolly.

"I thought you would, when I called the name."

"Well, sir, what farther have you to say?"

"Only that I consider the offer which has so long been made by the king for Roderick the Rover, or any of his officers, to be an exceedingly liberal one!"

"There is no occasion for speaking in riddles, sir. What proposition have you to make to me?" said Francis.

"Why, I suppose if my evidence is worth buying to the king, it must be worth silencing by you."

Francis thought of the matter for a few moments, and then said to the Englishman,—

"Lawrence, I do remember you. I remember to have nursed you with my own hands, when you were severely wounded, and your frame sunken under fever. Do you not remember that wound in your side, Lawrence Bray?"

"Yes, I remember you lent a helping hand in those days, but years of time have passed by since, and the sear only remains."

"You remember, also, the oath of our company, I suppose, by what fearful ties we swore to defend and protect each other, and never to give evidence, even in self-defence?"

"Yes, I remember all that, but we are not on board the Spirit of the Wave now, nor under the keen eye of that daring fellow, Roderick the Rover."

"You are resolved, then, to betray me, Lawrence?"

"Unless you make it worth my while not to do so."

"Well, I am only secretary of legation here, and must consult with my principal before I can make you any large offer. This I will do forthwith; and in the meantime be careful that you keep your secret, for if it is told to another, it becomes worthless to you, and I shall never bargain with you for silence."

"I'm always up for an honest trade," said the rascally seaman, as he bowed himself out.

Francis walked the apartment for nearly an hour after the Englishman's departure, in no enviable state of mind, turning over the matter as to how he had best conduct himself. He could not very well communicate with Lord William; besides, perhaps it was better not to disturb him with the subject at this crisis, if it was possible to get rid of the unfaithful rover who had threatened him. He remembered the man as having been one of the pirate crew who left them in the West Indies—a man whom he had always doubted, and who was exceedingly unpopular among his comrades, from his unreasonable cruelty, and many bad traits of character which he had displayed. He saw at once that he was completely in his power, as well as Lord William himself, and he was puzzled as to what course he should pursue in this perplexing dilemma.

At last he resolved to see Lord William, for he knew full well that he could not command money enough himself to satisfy the demand that the Englishman would make, and then it must be a heavy amount of gold that could counter-balance the rich offer made by the king for the detection of Roderick, or any of his officers, and which has already been specified in these pages. Therefore Francis, putting on some ordinary clothes, mounted a good horse, and dashed off for Calderon castle. A short time brought him to its drawbridge, and announcing that he wished to see the Lady Calderon's valet, he was admitted by the porter, who soon procured him an interview with Lord William.

"My lord——" began Francis.

"H-u-s-h!" said the disguised minister; "call me Roderick."

"I have some very important matter to speak of."

"Well, say on, I hear you."

"One of our old crew, in the Spirit of the Wave, has found me out in the city, and threatens to betray me."

"His name?" asked Roderick, scowling deeply.

"Lawrence Bray."

"Quarter gunner?"

"The same."

"That fellow you tended so long in sickness?"

"Yes, it is he."

"That man knew just enough to be a knave. I always thought it of him, and never trusted him further than I could see."

"We are in his power now, without doubt."

"Did you remind him of his oath, Francis?"

"I did, sire."

"What did he answer?"

"That he was no longer on board the schooner, nor under your eye!"

"We are indeed in his power unless we are prompt, and this we must be in every movement. I will get leave to go back to town with you; I will pretend that I wish to get some harness for the horses, as my lady will hawk to-morrow, and we will arrange matters on the way thither."

Roderick put on a plain suit of page's attire, without the colours of the Calderon livery, and attended Francis back to the city. It was near nightfall, and the English sailor had agreed to call at the office at sunset. They arrived but a few moments before the time, having agreed that the man should be enticed without the city walls that night by promise of reward, and then Roderick would deal with him. Scarcely had Francis resumed his dress, when the man came according to appointment.

"You are punctual," said Francis, "but I am equally so. It will be impossible for me to pay you the amount I propose here, lest there shall arise some suspicion from seeing you take the gold hence, but if you will meet me beyond the city walls at ten, and promise never to enter its gates again, I will give you a fitting reward."

"I will do so," said the Englishman; "but where is the spot?"

"At the ruins of the French villa, at the cross roads."

"I know the place, and will meet you there when you say."

"Very well, let it be ten o'clock, punctually."

"I will be there, depend upon me," replied the seaman.

"Good day, then, until we meet again."

"Good day," replied the man, as he turned and passed out.

As he left the office, Lord William, still in the page's dress, came out from an adjoining apartment, where he had purposely remained to notice the man, and walked the room thoughtfully for some minutes, when he turned to Francis, saying,—

"I see no other way but to *remove* this Lawrence Bray."

Francis said nothing, but understood the words fully.

"It is the first case of betrayal, or a threat to this effect that I have ever had. The rascals were holden by such fearful oaths and bonds that none of them ever before dared to dream of the thing. Why should this unlucky chance have turned up here? But no matter, it has come, and must be met. We shall be punctual, Francis, and meet the man at the ruins precisely at ten o'clock, and from there I shall ride back to the castle."

"I will have the horses ready, my lord, in good season," replied Francis.

"And you may place a pair of my best pistols in the holsters, Francis, and see that they are faithfully charged!"

"I will load them myself, my lord," replied the secretary, turning at once to execute these directions.

CHAPTER XVI.

" All night I lay in agony,
    In anguish dark and deep;
My fevered eyes I dared not close,
    But stared aghast at sleep;
For sin had rendered unto her
    The keys of hell to keep."

" A fearful deed, but one of necessity."

THE TWO HORSEMEN.—"HAVE YOU BROUGHT THE BLUNT, MESSMATE?"—THE THREAT OF BETRAYAL.—THE TRAITOR CONFRONTED.—HE IS TOLD OF HIS OATH, OF THE OLD ASSOCIATION.—LAWRENCE BRAY.—THE TRAITOR'S FATE.— GETTING UP WITH OUR STORY.—THE PAGE, RODERICK, AND HIS MISTRESS.— THE PARTIAL DENOUEMENT.

Two horsemen rode quietly out of the city gates that night a little before ten o'clock; the one apparently a Spanish gentleman; the other his attendant. Having cleared the gates, and escaped observation, they put spurs to their horses, and dashed off at a gallop, without drawing the rein, until they paused among the ruins of an old villa, built by a French gentleman many years before, and now in a state to afford quarter only for owls and banditti. Both dismounted, and throwing the bridles over the pommels of the saddles, left their well-trained horses as secure as though fastened by halters, for the Spanish cavalry horse never moves from the spot, when his rider leaves him in this manner, until led away. They soon after heard footsteps approaching the ruins, and in a few moments the English sea man stood before them. Lord William wore his cap over his eyes, and kept his face averted, that he might not be recognised unless it was necessary.

"Well, have you brought the blunt, mess-mate?" said he to Francis.

"No, Lawrence Bray, I have got no gold for you!"

"Then, by the God of Heaven, I will betray you; ay, here, before your own page!"

"Stay, Lawrence Bray, I want to remind you of that oath, which you so solemnly swore to, never to betray a comrade."

"I care not for all that nonsense. You have not kept your agreement, and now I shall claim the king's bounty."

As he spoke thus, the page slowly approached from one side, while the bright clear moon burst out for a moment from a passing cloud, and lit about the old ruin so distinctly that one might have read in a book. He uncovered his head, and threw his hair from his forehead, and looked the seaman full in the face. The man started as though a sword had pierced his side, and trembled in every limb of his body. He stammered for words, but failed to utter them.

"Lawrence Bray," said Roderick, in a deep tone, "I do not wonder at your trembling thus!"

"Captain!" said the man, in a tone of voice that indicated a feeling of relief at finding him a mortal man, and not a spirit.

"Ay, your captain of the Spirit of the Wave, and that is Francis, whom you also well remember. You remember, too, the oath you have taken of secrecy, and you remember well the penalty of treachery. You were with us long enough I think also to find out what my promise is worth, and I promised you, and every individual of our crew, that I would sacrifice my own life at any time to punish a traitor. You are a traitor, and now prepare for death; your time has come!"

The man's eyes rolled fearfully to the right and left, to see if there was no mode of escape, but Francis had drawn his sword and intercepted the only path that led from the walls that surrounded them. Seeing escape by flight impossible, he drew a pistol from his pocket, and was steadily raising it in a level with the head of his former captain, when he was anticipated, for Roderick fired and shattered his right arm, which fell powerless by his side!

"Spare yourself the struggle, Lawrence Bray," he said; "for you know full well that I am more than a match for any man that ever sailed under me. I have shattered that arm, but I could have sent the bullet through your heart with the same effort; but I preferred to give you time to ask forgiveness. Now down, sir, and pray for mercy from above, for I will show you none. Nay, not a word, or you lose the chance for prayer. Be quick, sir, and be concise."

The man knew whom he had to deal with full well; he knew that Roderick was one who kept his word. Still he ventured a few promises and even oaths that he would never reveal the secret, but to no purpose. He was told that one who would break such a trust and oath as he had taken did not deserve a second chance for life.

The rough, hardened sinner knelt upon the rude stones of the crumbling pile, and perhaps for the first time for twenty years, repeated the Lord's prayer. As the last words died upon his lips, a ball from the pistol of Lord William entered his brain, and he expired without even a struggle!

The pirate captain, the humble page, the proud minister, now all merged into the *man*, and Lord William Withingham stood over the dead body of the freebooter, and mused sadly upon the matter, his brow showing how troubled was the spirit within.

"Would to Heaven," he said, "that my lot had been cast in some more peaceable sphere. I had hoped that no more blood would be required at my hands, but how else could I protect Francis and myself? Besides, am I not equally bound by my oath as captain to punish all traitors? We should have been under arrest before to-morrow morning if this fellow had been set free. I thought over all this matter; there was no other way—he was unfaithful, and he is punished!"

"Francis!"

"My lord!"

"Let us remove this body, and bury it behind the walls."

The two took up the body of the freebooter, and soon placed it in a rude stone mound secure from sight.

Then, after a few moment's conversation, in which some other matters were referred to, each mounted his horse, and with a good night, rode off in separate directions,—Francis back to the city, and Lord William to the Calderon castle. This had occurred on the night previous to the hawking excursion to which we have referred, and on which occasion the banditti had made the attack on Lady Calderon and her hawking party. Lord William safely reached the castle and was admitted; and after attending to some trifling matters that were entrusted to his care, he retired to his pillow and slept; but, ah! it was anything but quiet sleep. Men who deal with such spirits as did Roderick the Rover, and look so lightly upon life and human gore as they must needs do, do not know the sweet untroubled sleep that blesses the pillow of the righteous. They do their deeds over again in their sleep, and suffer afresh.

The reader will remember that we left our *dramatis personæ* in a somewhat unpleasant situation. Lady Calderon turning, saw Roderick fall, and immediately checked her horse's speed, and turned back just in time to see the brigand breathe his last, while Roderick had fainted from loss of blood, and lay insensible upon the ground.

At this moment two of the servants reached the spot, and under their hands, and the Lady Calderon's directions, he was speedily resuscitated, and after swallowing a little wine from a flask, he was able to mount his horse, and ride slowly to the castle, which was now scarcely a half league off. The servants were directed to walk one on either side and aid in supporting him; and thus arranged, they rode on to the castle in safety. The best couch that the castle afforded was moved to the little ante-room that joined her own, every comfort that assiduous thoughtfulness could suggest was procured, and a surgeon retained in constant attendance.

With such care as this, no wonder that the page recovered with almost miraculous speed; and yet it seemed as though he would be willing never to completely recover again, so long as the sweet Lady Calderon would come so frequently to ask with her own lips how he was getting on, and send him so many delicacies that he knew were prepared by her own hands for him! Ah, the thought was delicious. It required no very prophetic spirit in Roderick to see what all this would result in. He now looked forward to success, if his good star would but continue to shine a little longer.

The same respect was observed by him towards the Lady Calderon as on the day of his first donning her livery, nor did the lady herself pass any bound of dignity in her intercourse, but still there was a gentleness of voice when she addressed him, a thoughtfulness for his feelings and comfort, that told a volume with every utterance; and then there is a language of the eye—that most expressive organ— that often speaks more honestly than the tongue, and never with less effect. These were the mediums thus far, through which the proud lady and the humble page had communed with each other; no word of mouth that the most scrupulous might question had been uttered.

Roderick was again restored to health, and to his office so near to the person of the Lady Calderon. Again he read to her, and again he went to the fields with her, but with more caution, venturing but to short distances from the castle, and avoiding the brigand's dell where they had before been attacked. Lady Calderon seemed to be ever with the noble-looking and handsome page. The neighbouring families noticed it, but slander itself did not dare to breathe aught against the fair fame of the Lady Calderon. How Roderick burned to declare his love, but he feared the plan was not quite ripe, and he had sworn to be married for himself alone; no one to whom he addressed himself should know of his wealth or even of his name—he must be loved for himself. In the instance of the Lady Calderon, he could hardly have tested her so well in any other way, for she belonged to a race, and was herself very proud in station, upholding the honour and credit of her ancient pedigree.

"Will my lady ride to-day?" asked the page, some two weeks after the occasion of his wounds having now quite recovered.

"Yes, Roderick, if you think you are strong enough to go," was the kindly spoken and considerate reply.

"I am quite recovered, my lady, I assure you."

"I have never thanked you for my brave and gallant delivery from the brigands, Roderick," said Lady Calderon, blushing, ay, and before her page! "You preserved me from a fate worse than death."

"I am more than repaid, my lady, in your kindness," replied Roderick, humbly.

"Speak not to me of that which is your right, Roderick, but rather name to me anything that I can do to serve you in return."

"Permit that I shall always remain in your service, and I am richly paid."

"Roderick! Roderick!" she replied, in a strange tone of voice, while a tear (a most unaccountable token) stole down her cheek!

"My lady," said Roderick, quickly, "have I offended?"

"In no way, Roderick," she replied, extending her hand towards him, while her face was averted.

The page dropped on one knee, and pressed it respectfully to his lips! We need hardly say that the ride for that afternoon was deferred, as the Lady Calderon seemed inclined to be alone in her own apartment, giving directions to her maid that she was not to be called or seen the rest of the day.

CHAPTER XVII.

"Look, Isabella,
I stand between thee and a life of sunshine.
Thou wert both rich and honoured but for me!
That thou could'st wed me, beggar as I am,
Is bliss to think, or clearly see how I rob thee.

FRANCIS FOLLOWING IN THE FOOTSTEPS OF HIS MASTER LITERALLY.—THE PLIGHTED TROTH.—A GRAND CELEBRATION FOR THE KING'S BIRTH-DAY.—THE DENOUEMENT INDEED.—"RODERICK, THAT HAND IS YOURS!"—THE INVITATION FROM THE KING, AND ITS RELUCTANT ACCEPTANCE.—RODERICK THE PAGE RETURNS TO THE CAPITAL.—THE PLOT THICKENS, AND THE READER GETS HOLD OF THE THREADS OF OUR PLOT.

NEAR the foot of a mountain that makes within a half league of the city walls of what was at the time of our story the capital of Spain, there is a little hamlet of vineyard dressers. All day long their time is employed upon the neighbouring hill-side, dressing and tending the vines, until the season of harvest, when they help to press out the delicious juice of the grape.

It was one mild evening about this date in our story, when a vintage maiden sat in the delicious breeze at the door of the cot. She was spinning industriously, while by her side there sat one seemingly a tradesman from the city, for he looked better dressed than those who inhabited the valley.

Never did Spanish peasant look prettier than did Imogene Perz, the vintage maid. Her dark, Spanish complexion was most beautifully tinged with the rich rose-coloured hue of health, her face was quite oval, and beautifully expressive. Her whole appearance bespoke the most unsullied innocence of heart, and she listened with increasing colour to the words of him by her side. There was no flattery in those words, they came warm from the heart of the speaker, and his fine, manly countenance showed that truth alone dwelt there. He was about the middle size, well formed, and wore a certain dignity and ease about his manner that showed he was no stranger to good company. He was talking of love to Imogene, and it was honest love, for the speaker was Francis, the secretary.

"Then you will promise to be mine, dearest?" he asked, as he encircled her waist with his arm.

"Yes, Francis, I promise, for I love no one else so well. I did love my dear mother so fondly, but she and father are both gone now, and I feel lonely indeed without a heart to confide in."

How prone we are to follow in the footsteps of those who are above us. Francis saw his master's plan, and determined to follow it. Already had he seen a lovely girl among the vines, and had even spoken to her. Her sweet simplicity and remarkable beauty attracted his eyes, and her sweetness of disposition afterwards his heart. She did not know whom he was, or whether he had a doubloon in the world. Her regard must indeed be honest if he could win it under such disguise, as to make him appear a poor man. And thus, taking example by Lord William, he adopted the coat of a poor man, and won her heart as such.

The king had issued his cards for a superb annual levee, and all the nobility were preparing for the occasion. It was the king's birth-day, and it was always made the occasion of great rejoicing. The Lady Calderon was invited, and indeed the king had so far honoured her above the rest, as to add a postscript to the illuminated invitation, soliciting her early attendance. The lady had received it one evening by an express courier, had read it, and now mused over its contents, when Roderick quietly entered the room. He had not seen her since the interview of the previous day, to which we have referred, and consequently felt in no slight degree embarrassed, but as was his custom, he asked,—

"Has my lady any commands this morning?"

"None, Roderick."

He turned to leave the room.

"Stay," she said, "how is your wound to-day, Roderick?"

"Better, my lady, better every day."

"I am very happy to know it," said Lady Calderon, evincing an interest that was too evident not to note.

"Your ladyship is so very thoughtful of my trifling hurt," he said.

"It was incurred in my service, Roderick, and it is but proper that I see you have all attention."

"True, my lady, you have done more than this."

She turned a languid and beautiful eye full upon him, piercing his very heart. He read his fate in that one glance; it spoke a volume to his heart, and he resolved to speak—now was the time. He approached her, as she reclined upon the couch with the royal note by her side; he knelt, and gently took the soft, white hand that hung listlessly by her side, and pressed it to his lips, saying,—

"Forgive, oh! forgive me, lady, if I offend, but the passion that consumes my very heart is so ardent for you that I forget all else."

She answered not, but the hand remained a willing prisoner within his own, while with the other she covered her face and sobbed with emotion.

"Speak to me, lady, oh! speak. Have the stories turned my head that I have read of olden time, when noble maidens have forgotten their high estate, and stooped to love when they have found a fond, devoted heart? Ah! lady, I can think of nothing save thee. I dream of thee, and my days are filled with thoughts of thee. For three months I have drank in the intoxicating sweets of your dear company, almost too much joy for me to share so freely; and now, forgetting my station and yours, I hold your hand thus boldly in my own!"

"Roderick, that hand is yours!"

"Do I hear aright?"

"'Tis the heart that speaks, the head condemns."

"Lady, and can you love an humble, low-born page?"

"Rank is as nothing, Roderick, when the heart is concerned, and I tell you frankly that mine is wholly yours!"

"But, lady, do you realize that to love me you must forswear all the rest of society? Who would permit the acquaintance of my lady's page, now her husband? Think, my lady, think of the sacrifice ere you rush blindly forward."

LAWRENCE BRAY SHOT BY LORD WILLIAM WITHINGAM.

"I have thought of all, Roderick, and my heart is yours!"

"But I can never hope to own your hand also?"

"You have won them both by your noble gallanty and devotion."

"But the world, my lady, heed what the world will say, for I would have no sacrifice of this nature without forethought."

Roderick had risen from his kneeling position, and now stood erect in all his nobleness of bearing. The page was gone, and the noble cavalier stood there in his place. He had forgotten his accustomed prudence in his earnestness; and Lady Calderon, who had never beheld him thus before, evincing the true character that so befitted him, that of a noble and commanding bearing, when she noted him now, was struck with admiration, and paused for a moment while she gazed upon him, and then said,—

"I know it all; but Roderick, they shall only prove to you how truly I love you, for it is not unmaidenly to speak of such feelings as prompt me now."

"Then, lady, henceforth I am your devoted companion, and the heaven of my wishes and prayers is more than realized. If a life of constant and unwearied devotion can in part repay the great sacrifice you make, then mine be the task."

"I have here an invitation from the king, Roderick, even his own signature; but to prove to you how truly I speak, I shall reject it, and from this moment discard society."

"Nay, dear lady, attend this, the last levee there, for it is the king's birthday, and all the nobility of Spain will be there."

"I have not the spirit to go, Roderick, and had rather not."

"If I may ask it, dear lady, I pray you go, at least this time."

"Well, if you wish it, Roderick, but it will be my leave-taking of the court and its brilliant circles." •

"I do not like to think that, dear Lady Calderon."

"Nay, I do not object to the sacrifice."

"May I order matters, then, for your ride to town this morning?"

"Yes, Roderick, as you wish it, I will go, and you can arrange the necessary matters as usual for this occasion."

Raising her hand again to his lips, Roderick left the room, and Lady Calderon mused to herself.

"Well, the Rubicon is passed, and I am the betrothed of the humble page! Who would have thought this of you, proud Lady Calderon? But I have acted wisely, for where the heart is, the hand should be also. From the first hour I saw him, heard him speak, listened to his reading, and gazed upon his noble figure, I loved him. Some peculiar chord of memory seemed touched, for which I could not account, but all is now resolved and fixed. I shall hardly miss the gay circles of the nobility, though by my own choice I shall be debarred from them, but such a heart as Roderick's can make amends for hosts of the gay and thoughtless votaries of fashion. No, no, I shall never repent my choice."

Saying which, she walked thoughtfully towards her dressing-room, after touching a bell for her maid. Her clothes were duly arranged for the assembly, herself prepared, and early in the afternoon she started for the city, leaving Roderick behind at his own request, and indeed as she herself would have suggested, lest some premature development of their affection should take place. Besides which she did not wish to expose Roderick in his present dress in the city, where they had never been together.

Hardly had the carriage and outriders disappeared from the sight of the castle, when Roderick mounted a favourite horse of tried spirit and bottom, and dashed off by a circuitous route to the city, which he seemed desirous to reach before the Lady Calderon should do so. By hard riding he was enabled to accomplish this, and as he passed the guard at the gate he turned, and in the distance could just discern the carriage and riders that accompanied the Lady Calderon. A smile of triumphant success lit up his fine countenance, and the next moment he dismounted in the court-yard of his own house. Handing his horse to a servant, he entered, and was soon engaged with Francis over the numerous papers that had accumulated since his absence. These disposed of, he gave Francis a few words of explanation, and then dressed himself in his dress of office as the English minister of the court of Spain, and at the usual hour, with all the ceremony and elegance that attaches itself to his office, drove in his own carriage to the royal palace, where a ready coined story, winding up with the haste that the minister had made on his long journey in order to greet his majesty on his birth-day, put the monarch in the very best of humours, and he shook the hand of Lord William cordially, then drawing his arm within his own, he walked familiarly with him into the grand reception room, where many of the guests were already assembled to greet his majesty on the occasion, eyeing Lord William with envy at the marked attention which he received from their royal master.

CHAPTER XVIII.

"What do I see?
Can these things be in stern reality?
Or do I dream while yet awake,
Surely, some spirit hath else possessed me."

LORD WILLIAM AT THE KING'S LEVEE.—MEETING OF THE ENGLISH MINISTER AND LADY CALDERON.—"RODERICK!"—"MY LADY!"—EXPLANATION TO THE KING.—REFLECTION UPON LAWRENCE BRAY.—NEWS FROM ENGLAND.—THE RESOLVE TO RETURN HOME.—THE LETTER TO LADY CALDERON, AND THE COURIER.

It will be remembered that at the close of the last chapter, we left Lord William Withingham arm-in-arm with his royal host on the occasion of the levee at the palace. The English minister had chatted thus with the king but a few minutes, when the Lady Calderon was discovered at the opposite side of the spacious apartment, surrounded by a large circle of friends and admirers. Lord William and the king had noticed her at the same moment, and both gazed upon her for a short time in silent admiration.

"Is she not very beautiful?" asked the king, at last.

"She is, indeed," said the minister, gazing upon her he loved with a swelling heart, and full of admiration.

"Of course you have been presented to her, my lord?" said the king.

"Never," replied Lord William, gazing still upon the Lady Calderon, completely absorbed in the contemplation of her loveliness.

"Is it possible?" said the king, in astonishment; "then come with me: for not to know the Lady Calderon is to be unknown of the sweetest lady in the realm."

The king paused for a moment, but still Lord William seemed lost in contemplation, and heeded him not.

"My lord," said the king, gently touching his arm.

"I beg your pardon, sire, I had nearly forgotten myself."

"Are you already in love with the Lady Calderon, my lord?"

"Nay, sire, but will you present me to her?"

"With all my heart," said the king; "come, let us see her at once, and recall your sleeping wits, my lord, for she will give you a test with her brilliant fancy and ready wit."

"True, very true," said Lord William, half to himself; "such beauty might well silence the boldest."

Saying which, the two, pausing only to return the polite salutations of the throng of noble ladies and lords through whom they were making their way, soon stood before the queen of beauty in that brilliant assembly. Of course, all gave way at the approach of the king and him who leaned familiarly upon his arm; and the king saluting her gracefully, presented Lord William Withingham as his excellency the English minister! The lady rose with graceful ease to give her hand to one so distinguished, when her eyes met those of Lord William. She paused for a moment, gazing full in that dearly beloved face. Could it be possible that such a resemblance existed, or had a miracle converted her page into a minister of state! The rich colour that bedecked her cheeks fled from them, and she was as pale as death, still gazing in silence. The king, bewildered at such a reception, looked alternately from one to the other in astonishment, while Lord William's heart was too full for utterance. At length Lady Calderon approached a step nearer, and said,—

"Roderick! speak, and break this awful spell!"

"My lady!" said Lord William, extending his hand.

The voice was enough; she could see through it all at a single thought now. She trembled for an instant, and fell fainting into the arms of the king, who bore her immediately to the queen's apartments hard by the drawing rooms.

The king soon returned to ask an explanation of Lord William, whom he found in a retired part of the saloons.

"My lord, what does this mean?" asked the king, gravely.

Lord William had already adopted his plan of procedure, and he replied with assumed indifference,—

"I had the good fortune to do her a service once, sire, on the road where she was attacked by brigands, and doubtless the memory of the event has shocked her for a moment."

"But you told me you had never been introduced to her."

"Nor was I, formally; she never knew me as the English minister."

"I see, I see," said the king; "romantic, very; possibly something may grow out—hey, my lord?"

Lord William turned the subject, after inquiring as to the situation of the Lady Calderon, and then both joined in the dance and festivities that surrounded them. The king, with light and boisterous spirits, enjoyed the hour to its full, while Lord William, with a beautiful Spanish maid in the waltz, seemed to be as much amused as his royal host, and thus the night wore away, until the Lady Calderon's coach was announced, when Lord William attended her from the queen's apartments to the carriage, whispering gently to her the while!

When Lord William returned to his apartments that night, he found that despatches had been received for him from home. He opened one letter after another, hastily glancing over their contents, until he came to one with a black seal; it announced the death of his father! Lord William did not bear his parent the affection that a son is generally supposed to possess for a father, for he had hardly been a father to him, but still he did drop a tear—a sincere tear of regret—and he was sad, too, at the thought that he was now alone in the world with neither mother, father, nor brother—all, all had gone for ever. Another letter from his father's attorney informed him that the property and possessions had all been left to him as the sole heir, and closed with a recommendation that he should return to England long enough to close up the business affairs of the estate, which was in an unsettled condition; and, as many thousand pounds sterling were involved in the matter, it would be for his pecuniary benefit to return for a period at least.

He turned to Francis, after reading this letter, and dwelling upon it for a few moments, said,—

"How should you like to make England your home, Francis?"

"Very well, my lord, indeed, I should far prefer it to Spain."

"Why so, Francis?" asked Lord William.

"To speak truly, my lord. I am in constant fear of being recognized here, and that you know would be certain death to me."

"A good reason truly; but how could you leave Imogene, of whom you have spoken to me?"

"She would go with me, my lord, to the ends of the earth," said the faithful secretary; "but excuse me, my lord, could you think of leaving the Lady Calderon behind you in Spain?"

"No, Francis, no; she must go with me if I go, or else I remain here at all hazard. I have letters here that may decide me to start within this month for England; this is the reason that I speak of these matters. I too have looked more seriously upon the matter of our being discovered for freebooters; my official dignity would count as nothing in that case, and we should both be sacrificed to the hatred of these revengeful Spanish rascals."

"It has been my fear night and day, my lord, constantly; and once we have been very near to the sacrifice, certainly."

"With that Lawrence Bray? Yes, that was a fortunate or unfortunate escape, either, for the man's death sets heavy upon my conscience, Francis. It was done in cold blood!"

"True, my lord, but it was positive self-defence."

"I don't know, Francis; villain as Lawrence Bray was, I wish I had given him the chance of his life in a duel, for it was the first time I ever took life in cold blood."

"You are too sensitive, my lord, you who have killed a score of men in a single hour upon the enemy's deck."

"That is far different, Francis, when the blood is up, and we fight for victory, when open war is declared, and your enemy falls with his weapon in his hand. That is different, very different, Francis, from coolly blowing a man's brains out."

"I can see no other sure way in which you could have protected yourself, my lord; the man was not to be trusted, and according to the bond and his oath, you were his executioner."

"I have tried to reason in this way also, Francis, but if ever I find it necessary to place myself against another of those men, it shall be on equal terms; he shall have the chance of his life."

"Would it not be best, my lord, to leave such a dangerous locality, where you are liable to be so unpleasantly situated."

"I have thought so lately, Francis, and therefore have given more serious attention to these letters."

"I am very glad of it, my lord, for I shall never be easy here."

"You are right, Francis, and I shall proceed at once to close up my affairs here, and send to England for permission to return."

"I am overjoyed to hear it, my lord."

"You may get out a horse, Francis, and as soon as the city gates open, take a letter I shall give you to Calderon castle. I will write it at once, and you will only have time to prepare yourself."

The willing secretary, though he had not slept at all, readily complied with his master's directions, while Lord William, burying his face in his hands, seemed lost in meditation. At last he drew his writing materials to his side, and wrote the following note to her he loved, the Lady Calderon. It was to tell her all, and ask for her forgiveness, and a renewal of the promises she had made to the page.

"To the Lady Calderon,—

"The secret is at last discovered, and I have now only to sue for your forgiveness. The humble (but devoted and happy) page, Roderick, is the English minister of the Spanish court, Lord William Withingham. I will not attempt to extenuate my conduct on paper, but will simply explain it to you. From the moment I first met you I became yours, heart and soul. I seemed to have known you before, so quickly did the chords of my heart vibrate at our meeting. I have scarcely thought of aught else for a moment since. When I looked upon you, and loved you so devotedly, the hope entered my bosom that I might win your heart, but I thought, after much dreaming, if this could be done by myself alone, untitled unheralded, then indeed I should have a test of affection which those can rarely, attain who fill the circle of life to which we were both born. I could see nothing unfair in the scheme I proposed, for if you heeded me not, surely you knew me not, and with a broken heart I should have retired; but if I succeeded and won the dearly coveted prize, your heart, as an humble, unpretending page, then you would love me none the less to find that I bore rank and title equal with your own. Thus I reasoned, lady.

"You were about leaving your castle, at the time of which I speak, for a distant province, to be absent some weeks. I also retired to the country, to study and to dream of thee. A moustache and page's dress, with some practice, soon made me at home in my new profession, besides sufficiently disguising me from any chance of discovery. My agent hired your page to leave you, and at the same time to recommend one who was his friend. I appeared; you took me, and I wore the Calderon livery. Oh! the sweet hours that I there passed, ever so near to you, reading to you, or serving you in some light and pleasant way; and then such gentle assurance of my acceptable services, such wealth of heart riches as I reaped in your dear smiles, and considerate promptings. Oh! lady, it came very near to my early thoughts of paradise.

"Well, the page and the mistress grew daily more intimate, all unwittingly on your part, but how consciously on mine! until, at last, fortune threw danger in your way, and then my good fortune placed me near to protect you; the brigands were repulsed, and my suit was won. You then told me that you loved me, poor, unknown, untitled, you loved and gave me your heart.

"May the nobleman claim of you the privilege you granted to the page?

"Devotedly yours,

"Roderick."

Francis galloped with this letter through the city gates as the morning gun was booming from the frowning battlements of the Spanish Citadel, and sped on his way towards Calderon castle.

CHAPTER XIX.

"Did she give thee aught for me?
A letter, boy,—why, hand it me quickly;
For I do famish for the food this may impart.
Ah, joy, ah, happiness—my cup is full!"

THE RETURN LETTER.—FRANCIS AND HIS SUIT.—THE MOONLIGHT WALK.—LORD WILLIAM AT CALDERON CASTLE.—THE SUSPICIONS OF THE RETAINERS.—A SPANISH WEDDING.—LEAVE-TAKING.—REFLECTIONS UPON THE QUARTER-DECK. —REVIEW OF HIS LIFE, TO THE PRESENT HOUR BY LORD WILLIAM.

Love is a strange passion. Lord William knew it well, and therefore he was not without fear as to the result of his suit with Lady Calderon. She who loved him as a page might have been actuated in no small degree by a feeling of romance, and by the tales she had read of olden time, when love used to level all rank, and lay the sceptre by the shepherd's crook. The force of time and circumstance might have powerfully combined to produce the feelings she evinced. She might have thus loved the page, when she would have passed unheeded the nobleman, in whom accomplishments are expected, as a matter of course. Besides all this, might she not blame him for the course he had pursued, the deception he had practised upon her? As he thought over these things, he almost trembled for the result, and the very hours were burthensome indeed, until Francis again returned. He met him at the door, and impatiently demanded the answer.

"It is here, my lord," said the secretary, handing the letter.

Lord William opened it, and read as follows :—

"MY LORD,

"Whether nobleman or serf, my heart is equally yours. From the hour of our first meeting I was struck with your appearance; I had hardly listened to your voice when it seemed that we were friends from childhood, and before a week had rolled over our heads after you came to the castle, my heart was wholly yours. In vain was the struggle of pride, my chains were woven of silk, and yet stronger than iron. I laboured not to evince the feelings that actuated me, but all in vain, and at last I told you all. And ah! the joy that filled my heart from that moment knew no bounds. I could almost cry with vexation that you are noble after all, for I might have shown you how lightly true love holds a title. I need say no more. This from—

"Yours, devotedly,

"IDA CALDERON."

If there was ever a happy man, Lord William Withingham was that man. He was half beside himself with joy. He pressed the letter again and again to his lips, asked Francis a thousand questions about the Lady Calderon, and bade him prepare a carriage for him to start for the castle.

A few hours, and Lord William and Lady Calderon sat side by side in the same apartments where he had so often waited upon her as page. Then he was habited as a menial—now, as a lord! Then he scarcely handed an article save on bended knees—now, his arm supported her waist! Then his words were chosen for their respectful utterance—now, he breathed into her ear the words of love!

"Ah! dear Ida, why should the world say 'the course of true love never did run smooth?'"

"Because of their ignorance, my lord, for I have seen perfect love in many a lowly peasant's cot."

"None that could equal ours, dear Ida."

"I am too much prejudiced to admit its possibility, my lord."

"But Ida, I have never heard you speak of your father."

"My father? He is long since dead," she replied, with a sigh.

"Dead, Ida? I thought he was only absent from home."

"No, my lord, he is dead these many years."

"But who is the Signor Calderon of whom the servants speak?"

"Ah! that is my uncle, and now I remember, you have never met; but he is a fine old fellow, and you will like him well. He was my guardian until I became of age, and now he does my land business for me."

"It had been reported to me that he was your father, Ida."

"No, only my uncle, though he has been a parent in kindness."

"Well, Ida, I have got to return to England, but I dare not hope you will go with me."

"To remain there, as a home?"

"Yes, Ida, my own castle awaits me—father, mother, brother, all dead, and the halls deserted save by menials."

"It will be hard for me to leave my birth-place here, but it would be a desert without you now, my lord."

"Will you give me that hand, Ida, before the priest, and afterwards embark for merry England?"

"Anywhere, my lord, so that I go with you," she said, as he drew her cheek to his own, and kissed it!

The uncle, Signor Calderon, was sent for to return to the castle; the servants were all set about preparing for their mistress's departure, and the king's reluctant consent was gained first for the solemn nuptials, and afterwards for the departure of the Lady Calderon with the English minister for his native land.

Francis, advised by his master of his intention to leave before long for home, also apprized the vineyard maiden, of whom we have before spoken. But though she loved Francis with all her tender and gentle heart, still it was harder for her, orphan as she was, surrounded only by the most common necessities of life, to leave her lowly cottage home at the mountain's base, than it was for the Lady Calderon to bid her palace home farewell. The industrious maiden had passed so many happy though busy hours beneath her humble shelter that she loved it, and the associations connected with it, more dearly than Lady Calderon could do her gilded apartments.

"Must we leave Spain, dear Francis?" she asked of her lover.

"Yes, dearest, there are many reasons why I must go."

"Then I must consent to go with thee, though I fear much my heart will hang about my early home."

"But you will be happy, dearest, I know, for the clime to which we go is a pleasant one, my occupation most agreeable, and I shall not be called away from thee at all."

"These things will make any place seem to me like home, Francis, but it is harder for us who have little to love save our homes, to leave them, than for the rich, whose wealth buys them other pleasures than the ties that industry plants and nurtures in the peasant's heart."

"You speak like a philosopher, my dear girl," said Francis, kissing away a tear from her cheek; "but I shall only endeavour the more strenuously to render you happy, knowing the feelings that actuate your gentle heart. Love reconciles us to nearly any change, dearest, and I am sure I could be happy with you anywhere."

"Oh! I too feel this, dear Francis, but still it would be untruthful not to speak my whole heart to you."

"I know its wealth, dear girl, and shall treasure it," he replied.

And the two, walking side by side, along the mountain road, looked down upon the little village that lay sleeping under the brilliant moonlight of the night. It was very still, that mountain road, and they talked of love, and promised to meet before the altar on the coming day.

Signor Calderon came in due time. He guessed the errand upon which he was sent for, and he willingly lent his aid in furtherance of the design of his noble niece. He was sorry to have her leave her ancient home, but he reasoned that all was for the best, and he would himself give the bride away before the altar. It was arranged, also, that he should remain in charge of the castle and tenantry, accounting to Lady Calderon for the proceeds until she should return again to Spain. All these matters duly arranged, Lord William's letters of recall received, his passport granted, and his affairs regularly closed up, the wedding was to take place, and then they were to embark for England.

Lord William had been passing the day with Lady Calderon about this period, when as night approached, he mounted his horse to return to the city. As he passed through the portals of the castle to the draw-bridge, he heard the servants say,—

"Did you ever see such a resemblance as my lord, the English minister bears to that Roderick, my lady's page, who disappeared so suddenly not long since?"

"I have thought of it a dozen times," said another.

"The figure is the very same," said a third, "the countenance and all, but then it can't be, and that puts an end to the matter."

"I don't know," said the butler, cunningly; "Antoine, who has returned to his

SHE LISTENS TO THE WORDS OF HIM BY HER SIDE.—*See page 72.*

post again, looks very wise at times, though he does not say anything. If it was not for fear of offending my lady, I think I could throw some light upon the matter."

Lord William was now just passing out of hearing, and turning, he thought he would stop the gossip where it was—so he rode back a few paces, and saying a kind word to the porter and butler, with those about them, he tossed a purse to be divided among them, and rode on over the draw-bridge.

"Page, peasant, or king, he's a gentleman," said the butler, as he counted out the broad pieces, and divided with the rest, keeping the lion's share for himself.

"How well he sits on his horse," apostrophised the contented porter; "he would keep this gold piece in the stirrup 'neath his toes for a league, at a hard gallop. Come, boys," he continued, "up with the bridge, there will be no more passing to-night."

It is hard to conceive the splendour of a Spanish wedding without having witnessed one; and on the occasion of Lord William Withingham's marriage with Lady Calderon, neither ingenuity nor expense were spared to render it unrivalled in magnificence. Even the king expressed his surprise at the lavish expenditure that had been made, but what did it matter to either of them? The lady's wealth was princely in its extent, and Lord William, as we have already seen, was possessed of an amount which, to say the least of it, would equally match the lady's. Francis, too, was married at the same time, and with the same ceremony, one benediction making both couples man and wife.

This done, it only remained for my lord and lady to make their parting calls, and give one superb entertainment, ere they prepared themselves for the voyage to England. Two happier brides and bridegrooms never swore to love each other than were this happy party.

The king warmly pressed Lord William's hand at parting, saying that his royal master could never send one so welcome to his court as he had been; and receiving the kind farewells of all, the English minister embarked for home.

When he was seated upon the quarter-deck of the vessel that was to bear them over the sea, he reviewed for a moment the few last eventful years of his life. He glanced at his year of roving in the West Indies, his singular success as a freebooter, his engagement with the government as a privateer, his good fortune in that capacity, and finally his kind reception at court, and appointment to the most desirable court in Europe as minister, his intimacy with his former enemy, the king of Spain, his near likelihood of discovery, the summary punishment he had inflicted upon Lawrence Bray, his plot upon the affection of Lady Calderon, his life as a page, his success in winning her affections, their sumptuous and gorgeous marriage, their determination to return to England, their embarkation,—all, all, crowded themselves upon his mind in succession, until he seemed confused with the flood of thought that deluged his brain. He seemed almost inclined to consider it all a dream; but no, stern reality stared him in the face, and he was forced into conviction. He gazed on the Spanish coast thus musing, until the hills and vales faded away in the dim distance.

CHAPTER XX.

"Her flag—I had no glass, but fore and aft,
Egad! she seemed a wicked looking craft;
But nearer come across the rippling seas,
Her red flag flaunted in the fresh'ning breeze."

GOOD-BY TO MADRID.—FEARFUL REVENGE OF PIRATES.—FEARFUL SCENE FALLEN IN WITH AT SEA.—A DESERTED FELUCCA.—PARALLEL CASE IN MODERN TIMES. —THE STORM AND THE STRANGE SAIL.—THE MYSTERY SOLVED.—THE ENEMY A ROVER.—THE GUN AND THE BLOOD-RED FLAG.

MADRID and all the splendour of the Spanish court were left behind, and the party, consisting of my Lord and Lady Withingham, Francis and his wife Imogene, and Antoine, the faithful valet, who had given up his place near the perso of Lady Calderon to accommodate Lord William, were swiftly borne on their way over the sea to the shores of England. Never was there a happier party on ship-board, but still it seemed as though destiny was against them, for another adventure crowded itself upon Lord William's already over-charged history.

Scarcely had they cleared the Spanish coast when they fell in with a singular felucca-rigged craft, which the tide and wind nearly drove a-foul of them; but by adroit management, the vessel in which the party had embarked got to windward of the felucca, which gave no tokens of being manned at all. At the suggestion of Lord William, a boat was lowered into the sea, and himself and a few seamen boarded the craft, not without some difficulty, however, as she was drifting free before the wind; but at last they succeeded, and gained her deck in safety.

The first man who ascended the side had no sooner raised his head above the bulwarks of the felucca, so that he could command a view of her deck, than he uttered a cry of horror, and fell back upon those behind him, telling them to get into the boat as soon as possible.

"Steady, there," said Lord William, who sat in the stern of the boat; "what are you afraid of? Does the bare deck of a felucca alarm you?"

"No, your honour," replied the man, pale with fear, who had first ascended the side; "but there is an awful sight there, sir."

"What is it, sir? Speak out, we have no time to lose."

But the man remained mute, as if stricken dumb with horror, while the rest of the crew refused to go up the side.

"Stand back, then, and let me go first," said Lord William; and in another moment he had sprung lightly up the side of the singular craft, and now paused upon the bulwarks, but little less astonished than the man had been to whom we have first referred.

The felucca seemed stripped of every valuable or useful article about the deck, upon which, nailed down by their hands and feet, lay some half dozen bodies, evidently but a short time dead. The deck was strewed with blood, and gave tokens that a fierce contest had been fought there. The sight of death in nearly all its forms was no new thing to Lord William, but the horrid sight of the mangled corpses was a degree beyond even his experience.

With a voice that admitted of no denial, he ordered the boat's crew on deck, and releasing the bodies, had them properly sewed up in hammocks, and buried in the sea. In the meantime, the sails of the felucca were so trimmed that she easily kept company with the Bristol Trader (the name of the vessel in which they had embarked for England), and Lord William had ample time to arrange matters to his liking. After decently burying the bodies, he examined the craft, and found such tokens as convinced him that she had been attacked and carried by pirates, who, after stripping her, had abandoned the vessel as unavailable to them; and doubtless exasperated at the resistance they had met with, had revenged themselves upon the bodies of their captives by the cruel treatment we have mentioned. It is hard to conceive of such an extent of brutality as can lead men to do such fearful deeds upon unresisting and lifeless corpses; such a thing seems to be almost impossible, yet we can bear testimony to an instance of precisely the same character, which has occurred as lately as the year 1828, somewhere between the capes of Virginia and the Bahama Banks. A vessel freighted, if our memory serves us right, at Kennebunk Port, Mobile, had made a passage to Havana, and was homeward bound with a cargo of molasses and sugar, when she was boarded by pirates, who being resolutely opposed by the brave Yankee captain and his crew, at last, after losing several of their own number, conquered. After despatching, as they thought, all the crew, they nailed their bodies to the deck, and stripping the brig of all available goods, left her to drift on the high seas. By cunning management, the mate of the brig, just before the pirates gained the victory, retired and hid himself in a secret place, and after they had disappeared, he again sought the deck, trimmed the sails as well as he was able, and steered the vessel into the track of the traders from the north and south, and was thus picked up in a few days after. The man is still living in New England, and the event to which we refer is still fresh in the memory of many individuals.

Lord William, after performing the duty of a Christian upon the bodies of the crew which had manned the felucca, made signal to the Bristol Trader, and leaving the vessel with her sails and helm set to carry her towards land, returned to his own ship. There the fearful story was told concerning the felucca, in the cabin truthfully and correctly, but in the forecastle with such exaggerations as made the stoutest tremble.

It was mid-day when Lord William returned to the ship, and scarcely had the look-out aloft lost sight of the felucca, before the always exciting cry at sea, of,—

"Sail O !" was repeated on the quarter-deck.

The captain who had been listening to the story of Lord William in the cabin, was on deck in an instant, and with trumpet in hand, demanded,—

"Where away ?"

"Off the weather beam, sir; you can't get her yet on deck sir, but I think she is rising."

"I see nothing but the indications of rough weather close there to windward," said the captain to Lord William who now appeared on deck,

Lord William took the glass and levelled it with a practised hand, and after but a moment's gaze replied,—

"There is a small craft hanging on the skirts of that squall, which is coming down hand-over-hand." .

"Ah, I see now," replied the captain after a moment's examination, but you must have a quick eye, my lord.,'

"It has been practised," replied the passenger and at the same time turning his eyes aloft he observed, "you had better be handling some of your lighter canvass aloft, get it in lively sir, for it is coming on."

These words of caution were not given one moment too soon, for before the upper sails were fairly brailed, the squall broke over the ship with a tremendous power, causing her to careen almost on her beam ends, but Lord William was on the quarter deck and taking the helm, with calm self-possession put the ship before the gale and soon placed the noble fabric in safety. He was at home again when battling with the elements !

The Bristol Trader flew like a bird before the wind, completely shut in by the clouds of spray and thick weather that swept along with her, until at last the clear blue sky broke over their heads again, and gradually the atmosphere, rarified by the fierce convulsions it had just experienced, became clear and the mist lifting as if by a charm, discovered the forgotten sail that had been made out far to windward at the commencement of the squall now but a short half mile astern, flying like the Bristol Trader before the wind under bare poles, not a stitch of canvass being visible. Indeed so small a craft could not have lived a moment steering any other course in such heavy weather. She was an English built schooner of about one hundred and twenty tons, sharp and narrow constructed for speed, and her trim and the manner in which she was managed and kept close in the storm, showed her to be well managed. Everything being now snug and secure on board the ship, the captain and Lord William had ample time to examine the stranger. Both did so for a long while, when Lord William spoke.

"Captain, have you got arms on board the ship ?"

"Arms ! my lord," said the astonished captain.

"Yes, guns, pikes, pistols, and a few tools of that sort."

"Why, yes, we have some arms, my lord; but why do you ask ?"

"Because, unless I am mistaken, we shall have need of them."

"Do you think yonder schooner looks suspicious ?"

"She is a rover, or else her looks sadly belie her. However, there is no danger while this sea runs, for she does not dare come near us for fear of swamping; but if you have an arm chest, it would be well to throw it open, and prepare for defence."

The captain of the Bristol Trader was no coward, but still he was taken a little aback at first, for although the quick and practised eye of Lord William detected the peculiar signs which he himself had more than once adopted in his life at sea, yet the slower intellect or suspicion of the captain had not yet been awakened by the strange sail that was now so close upon them. The measures, however, recommended by Lord William were promptly adopted, and arms were distributed to the men, with directions to put them in proper order. In the meantime, Lord William descended to the cabin, and calling Francis on one side, together they prepared their pistols and side arms for service.

In the meantime, the weather gradually moderated, and the sea went down as the night set in, and a clear, brilliant moon lit up the ocean far and near. The Bristol Trader was again covered with canvass from her topgallant to the deck, and her course was again laid by the compass homeward bound. The suspicious schooner still held her own, and as the ship spread her broad wings to the breeze, so did she set her sails, one by one, until both sped freely over the sparkling, moon-lit waters, now seemingly sleeping after their tumult. Lord William could easily see that the schooner, with the present wind, might outsail the ship if the master of her actions desired it, and therefore he was still more confirmed in his belief of her character, as her sails were not all spread, it being doubtless their object to hold the ship in sight until daylight, when, probably, it was the plan for them to engage the ship. This delay gave Lord William time to instruct the crew in their duty and make all proper arrangements to receive the pirates, for such he was now convinced they were, and he was engaged without intermission in drilling the crew of the Bristol Trader in the use of the arms, to which they were quite unaccustomed. Daylight at last appeared, and as it did so, additional speed was given to the schooner by spreading all her canvass, and as the sun burst up from the eastern horizon, it seemed to have acted as a match on board the Rover, for at the same moment, the report of a cannon came across the water, and a cannon ball skimming along the surface of the sea, sunk at last close by the ship.

All doubts as to the character of the schooner were now banished, for a flag with a blood-red flag was run up at the same time that the gun was fired from her deck.

CHAPTER XXI.

"Sharpen your blades,
And cut home, my boys, for more than life
Depends upon your bravery.'

COMMENCEMENT OF THE FIGHT.—HAND TO HAND.—"IN GOD'S NAME WHO ARE YOU?"—STRANGE RECOGNITION OF OLD SHIPMATES.—"REVENGE, REVENGE."—SINGULAR CLOSE OF THE BATTLE.—WITHDRAWAL OF THE PIRATES.—MUTINY AMONG THEM, SEEN FROM THE DECK OF THE BRISTOL TRADER.—THE FEARFUL FINALE OF THE BUCCANEER CREW.—REFLECTIONS.

THE schooner was soon abeam with the Bristol Trader, and the fight commenced in good earnest. There was no cannon on board the ship, but Lord William took good care that the small arms should be double-shotted and placed in the most effective hands. He knew from old experience that Francis was a perfect marksman, and a man was placed with a couple of guns to keep one loaded

for his use ; in this way he had only to watch his chance for a good shot, and then **he** was sure to lay one of them dead upon their deck. The crew of the ship were so placed that the cannon of the schooner could not harm them, and although the pirates kept the only two they had on board the pirate craft well-served, yet they did little harm save to the hull and rigging of the ship, while Lord William and Francis, both capital shots, were making fearful havoc among the pirates by their fatal accuracy with their small arms. The rovers began to realize this, after losing some eighteen of their number, and determined to board the ship at all hazards without further delay. They therefore ran close under the larboard quarter of the ship, and a score of them scrambled on board, sword in hand. They were resolutely met by the crew, headed by Lord William, Francis, and the captain, who either drove them into the sea, or lay them dead upon the deck ; this bloody reception did not seem to cool the fire of the pirates, who again luffed and threw a still greater number on board the ship. Their arrangements were better made this time, and several of the ship's crew being now wounded and two dead, they were enabled to effect a footing on the deck, but not without losing several of their number. All was smoke and confusion on the deck of the Bristol Trader, and the faces of the combatants were hidden from each other by the smoke of the powder fired from the pistols every few moments.

"Follow me to the quarter deck !" cried the leader of the rovers, having been driven forward by the combined efforts of the ship's crew.

"Stand firm," said Lord William to those about him, "mark your man as they come on, and fire upon him."

"Forward," said the rover captain, rushing up with his followers towards the foot of the main-mast, where Lord William and the crew of the Bristol Trader were standing. But the rovers tried in vain to break through the line of pikes that were ranged across the deck, while one of their own number was falling every moment from the steady aim of Francis and Lord William.

Such an encounter could not continue long, and the pirates, feeling that everything depended upon their promptness, made a bold push and broke the line opposed to them, coming to a hand-to-hand fight.

"Down with the rascals !" cried Lord William, cutting among the rovers with his sword most fatally to life and limb.

"Victory or death !" cried the pirate chief, approaching Lord William. The face of each was now completely blackened with powder, but you could have known Lord William by his noble bearing, his prompt and brilliant, as well as fatal use of the sword. The rover seemed to single him out as the leader, and indeed he had taken the lead, for the captain was overawed by his bearing and prompt action, and only sought to do his part in the fight.

"Hold, or you die !" said the pirate, with uplifted sword.

The thrust was skilfully parried by Lord William, who at the next moment ran one of the enemy through the heart with his sword, and then turned again to confront the leader of the crew.

"Hold," said the pirate captain to his men, "fall back I say !" The men obeyed in silence, and there was a pause in the fight.

"In God's name, who are you ?" asked the pirate captain of Lord William, after gazing at him a moment.

"Do you yield ?" asked Lord William, taking no notice of the question addressed to him.

"I never saw but one arm that fought thus," said the pirate, as if to himself.

Lord William gazed for a moment upon the man as if he had read him through all the powder on his face, then as if satisfied, said,—

"And that man, was Roderick Harrol !"

"It was Roderick the Rover."

"And you are Pierre Lancellette."

"Captain !" said the astonished rover.

"Pierre, send away these blood-hounds ; we can understand each other better alone !"

"Fall back—fall back, I say," repeated Pierre to his crew, who now crowded about him. "On board the schooner! I will arrange matters here. Back I say—what do you linger for?"

"Revenge, revenge," shouted a half dozen voices at once.

"Fall back, I say," continued the captain, "or I will make an example of some of you!"

The men looked first at each other, then at their dead companions, more than a score in number, then slowly, and muttering, turned towards the deck of the schooner.

"Well, Pierre," said Lord William, "I do not know but I might have expected this from the apprenticeship you served in the West Indies; but I little thought we should come together thus."

"It is odd enough, captain; I had lost all sight of you, as had all the rest of our old mess. Are you only a passenger here?"

"That is all; homeward bound to England, from Madrid."

"Madrid! You from Madrid? Why, I should as soon think of taking up quarters in the Admiralty office. Spain never had a more dreaded enemy than you, and here you have been eating salt, perhaps, with her king."

"All in the way of business, Pierre. But now let us understand each other. Are you disposed to haul off, and leave the Bristol Trader to pursue her course, or have I got to fight you a little longer before you make up your mind?"

"My mind is made up, captain, at once. You go unmolested by me, but I shall have hard work to restrain those fellows of mine. You once spared my life when I had attempted yours; now I can in some degree repay the debt, for you will acknowledge that I should take you at last."

"I never acknowledged such a thing, Pierre, I think you can bear me witness; and you would not get this ship while there was a man to fire a gun or wield a sword."

"Other motives than fear move me, captain. I should like to talk over old affairs. But I must hasten, or there will be rank open mutiny on board my schooner, for you have used us roughly."

Thus saying, Pierre Lancellette bowed, and turning from the deck of the ship, sprang lightly on board his vessel, at the same moment giving an order for cutting loose the grapnels that had bound the schooner to the ship. A few moments more, and the pirate craft tacked and stood to the north-west, being the opposite direction from the course that the Bristol Trader was on. Those on board the ship could see that there was much dissatisfaction on board the schooner at the manner in which the captain had seen fit to close the battle; and Lord William could see with his glass that the crew were in a state of open rebellion, that the officers were drawing close together on the quarter-deck for protection from each other, while the men were also drawn together at the main-mast. Though he could not hear him speak, he could see Pierre Lancellette addressing them, and soon after saw the men make a bold push, as if to clear the quarter-deck!

"Pierre will master them," said Lord William to the captain of the ship, who stood by his side, watching the pirates through a glass.

"He cannot make headway against such odds," replied the captain.

"My life for it, he will conquer them one way or another; he knows his trade too well to give in to them a single inch," continued Lord William, deeply interested in the scene he was watching.

"Sir," said Francis, who though slightly wounded, still kept on deck to watch the schooner, "the officers are all down! Pierre is killed, I think; he is not there!"

"I see him now," cried Lord William. He is cutting right and left; how he scatters the rascals! By Heaven, I wish I was by his side, just to help the cause of discipline," continued Lord William, nervous with the excitement that moved him.

"He has cleared a path to the cabin door, said Francis.

"Yes, there he goes into it," said the captain.

"Like a brave fellow," said Lord William, wrought up by old recollections, "he has gone to show them that he will conquer though he perishes in the attempt."

Scarcely had these words escaped the mouth of Lord William before a mountain of fire, smoke and missiles burst into the air, with a report that was deafening, even on board the ship, causing the Bristol Trader to tremble in every timber! The rover captain, seeing that his crew was about to gain the victory, had deliberately put a match into the magazine, and blown every soul into eternity in an instant of time!

"I knew it," said Lord William, thoughtfully, "he had the true spirit of a buccanneer. Captain," he continued, turning to him by his side, "I have fought in the same ship with that leader; he was a brave man."

Then turning his eyes from the spot, where nought now remained but the small fragments of the wreck, he walked the quarter-deck, absorbed in thought, for nearly an hour. The few past hours had made a deep impression upon him, with their fearful termination. At last Francis approached and interrupted him, saying,—

"Your lady, my lord, sends to ask why you are so long away?"

"Ah, yes, I had forgotten myself, Francis. I will join her immediately; go below, and say so to her."

"I will, my lord."

And after composing his thoughts, which had been roaming all through the chequered scenes of his life, reflecting upon the fearful fate of Pierre, of his former connection with him as a freebooter, of his dead parents and that cold-hearted brother who had been the cause of banishing him from his home—of the Golden Valley and the Isle of Man—of his entering the regular service—of his meeting with Paul Jones, with whom he had exchanged swords at parting; all these things he dwelt upon, and reviewed, and to himself, too, he made a vow that if he was permitted to reach his early home, he would repent of his reckless life, and endeavour to atone in some degree for its evils, by doing good in future, and relying upon the mercy of an all-gracious Parent. We say he thought thus, and after composing himself, went below to Lady Withingham, to relate the battle and its strange finale.

CHAPTER XXII.

"Sit still and hear the last of our sea sorrow."—*Shakspere.*

IDA.—A CONVERSATION THAT LOOKS LIKE BRINGING ON A DISCOVERY.—SIGNOR MATTENEZ.—THE SPIRIT OF THE WAVE, AND THE SINGULAR DISCOVERY OF THE MYSTERY.—A LAPSE OF YEARS, AND A MERRY MEETING AT THE OLD CASTLE.—THE ISLE OF MAN.—THE TRUE REPENTANCE.—NOTE FROM PAUL JONES'S PRIVATE JOURNAL.—THE AUTHOR'S FAREWELL.

DURING the fight, the females, with a single sentinel posted at the door, had remained close in the cabin, under fearful suspense for those who were dearer to them than life. At the close of the contest, Lord William had descended, but it was only for a moment, to assure his lady that he was safe, and also to press her to his breast, with a prayer of thankfulness that she was free from danger. But he had now come down to relate the particulars of the scene. He found Ida in tears, but they were tears of joy at his safety. She listened with deep interest to his story, and when they were at last quietly sitting side by side in the cabin, she said,—

"Dearest, neither of us has ever disclosed to the other the story of our early lives. What better time can there be than now?—for I have a matter that weighs heavily upon my mind."

"I have loved your presence so dearly, Ida, that I have scarcely roamed back to the past in my mind," replied her husband.

RODERICK, FROM THE DECK OF THE BRISTOL TRADER, WITNESSES THE DESTRUCTION OF THE PIRATES.

"When I heard your voice amid the din and conflict on deck, during the fight, as you gave your orders and cheered on the men, I was almost sure I had heard you do the same thing before."

"Impossible, Ida."

"Were you ever in the West Indies, dearest?" she asked.

"The West Indies, Ida,—yes; why do you ask?"

"Because I, too, have been there!" she replied, meaningly.

"Is it possible! What do you mean, Ida, by these words?"

"I scarcely know myself, but a strange light seems to be breaking in upon my mind—stranger because it has never been realized before."

As she spoke, she parted the hair from his forehead, and gazed full into his noble and handsome face.

"Speak, for heaven's sake," said Lord William; "what do you mean by these words, Ida?"

"That I now know you to be Roderick the Rover!"

"What strange chance has given you this intelligence?" asked Lord William, in amazement.

"Do you not remember Signor Mattenez, in the Golden Valley?"

"I do, indeed. How strange all this is—go on, speak at once of what you would say, for I too begin to see a new light."

"Signor Mattenez and Ida Calderon are the same!"

"Can it be possible I have been so dull, and now that you speak I so fully realize the whole truth?"

"Why is it any more strange than that I should not have known you? Once there was a passing thought crossed my mind, but I scouted it at once, for how could Roderick the Rover be the accredited minister of England to the court of Spain? Yet it ever seemed to me that I had heard your voice before; and when in the din of battle I heard it to-day, I was sure of the fact."

"But I never even suspected Signor Mattenez to be other than a young cavalier."

"When we left Spain, my mother and myself, it was thought best that I should assume the dress I wore and another name; and once dressed in this style, of course there was no change possible, and after my mother's death I became in some degree reckless. You remember, of course, when I left you. I went forthwith to my uncle's plantation. He received me kindly, and made me share freely the comforts of his home. Well, circumstances at last occurred at home in Spain, that proved my father's innocence beyond a doubt; and the king, anxious to make all the amends in his power, learned my location, and sent a special message to bring myself and uncle back to Madrid, and then reinstated me in all the wealth of our noble family; and in its enjoyment you found me at Calderon castle."

"Why, this would equal the Arabian Nights, Ida."

"Yet it is all true, as you yourself can bear witness."

"Did you not fear discovery in the Golden Valley?"

"At times I did, but then I thought of your noble character, and banished all fear from my heart."

"Dearest Ida," said Lord William, kissing her fondly.

"There was one time when I feared that I was discovered; for I had been bathing at what I thought a sufficiently secluded and protected place, when, as I had concluded my bath, I beheld you looking at me as if you had discovered all."

"To what do you refer?" asked Lord William, earnestly.

"To an evening bath on the shore."

"Where the trees approach so near to the beach?"

"Yes, that was the spot."

"God of Heaven! can it be possible, then, that you are the Spirit of the Wave?"

"It is very sure that I thought you had discovered me!"

"Why, what a blind fool I have been in everything that concerns you, dear Ida."

"Nay, not so bad as that, dearest, for you carried on your game of page to perfection."

"Be these things as they may," said Lord William, "I am quite happy that I possess you now," and as he spoke he drew her light and graceful form to his breast, and pressed his lips to her cheek.

It was a fine, clear, moonlight night, to which we wish to call the attention of the reader. It might have been a couple of years subsequent to the period of which we have just been speaking. The dark shadows of the noble castle of the Withinghams reached to the very entrance of the woods. Within those grey old walls there was a gay feast. It was the second anniversary of the wedding day of William Withingham and his beautiful wife. A little boy, scarcely a year old, was smiling and cooing in a nurse's arms near the seats occupied by Lord and Lady Withingham. It was their own! What a throng of happy faces was there assembled. There were Levi Belt and his beautiful wife, Grace Martin; there were Francis and Imogene, also married; and rarely, if ever, was there so truly joyous and happy a company before assembled. And now they pledge each other in bumpers, and Lord William tells them all a story, prefacing it by saying that it was strictly true, and that even he himself had been guilty of being its author. It was of the trick he had served the king, when he had tried to use him to the end of gaining his own selfish object. Of course, he suppressed the true names, but Ida understood to whom he referred, and the rest shrewdly guessed the truth.

Lord William at the castle, where also Francis was retained as a director of the tenantry, Levi Belt and his dear wife, Grace, with a little curly-haired boy and girl, to unite them still more closely to each other, and the happy fishermen that were so well cared for by the landlord, all together made up a happy settlement on the Isle of Man. Lord William, who had so long been accustomed to excitement, had recourse once in a while to daring and active service to satisfy his old habits.

There were parts of the island still frequented by the smugglers between France and the neighbouring shores, and Lord William, with Francis and his servants, more than once attacked and completely disbanded them, until the English government lending their assistance, the evil was thoroughly abolished. The island was about the same time joined to the English crown, and thus became a part of Great Britain. The cunning Lords of the Admiralty saw at once that it would form an excellent depot for the ships of war, and extensive yards and coves were built, and military barracks raised, and the place made in no small degree a military and naval depot for the army and navy of England. And at this day it looks more like a thriving sea-port city than an isolated isle. Fine roads and beautiful gardens are sprinkled in all directions, and it is noted among travellers for being a gem of commercial and national enterprise. The Withingham castle, or rather its ruins, still remain, and are frequently visited by the curious. The descendants of the family having removed to the main land, the better to enable them to participate in the service of government, filling as they do, high and important stations in the kingdom.

The closing years of Lord William's life were those of a true Christian, and he sought to educate and bring up his children in the fear of Heaven, and the love of the pure and good. His early life, for which we could adduce many, very many, palliating circumstances, was deeply and painfully repented of, and the utmost care was taken that his own offspring should have no influence to actuate them to misanthropic feelings, or unholy promptings; and thus they grew up around him and his dearly loved Ida, a source of honour and pride—offspring to whom he would cheerfully confide the honourable title and name of his house in keeping.

In the private journal of that great commander, Paul Jones, one of the bravest men that ever sailed a ship, there is the following narrative of the meeting with our hero off L'Orient.

"——— It was a hard fight, the most obstinate, I think, that I ever participated in, but the finale, the close, and all the incidents were equally peculiar. Conquered by the superior weight of the enemy's metal, I was obliged to yield, but only to be reassured that my sword was my own, and my vessel, too, all that was left of her. This Lord William Withingham had been a freebooter in the Spanish West Indies, where he had learned his trade so well that he could conquer any craft a third his superior in appurtenances and fittings. We related a few of the incidents of our eventful lives to each other in my cabin, over a glass of wine, and he left me, after making an enduring impression upon my memory of his bravery and gallantry. I heard of him afterwards, when he took a large French ship, better manned and armed than his own craft, which was most appropriately named the Spirit of the Wave."

And here ends our story, kind reader, in which we have striven to amuse and entertain you. The manner in which each successive chapter has been received, has cheered us on from page to page, until it has been far from an unpleasant employment for our leisure hours, thus to weave for you the threads of romance into tangible form.

Now, how well we should like to take you each by the hand, while we say, God bless you all!

THE END.